If They Hadn't Invented Golf...

We Never Would Have Needed
the Damned
Whisky

Bob Sheppard
3/2014

BOB SHEPPARD

ISBN: 1479214590
ISBN 13: 9781479214594
Library of Congress Control Number: 2012916916
CreateSpace Independent Publishing Platform
North Charleston, South Carolina

Dedication

TO MY FAMILY TREE

BOTH THE ROOTS AND THE BRANCHES

CONTENTS

GOLF AND WHISKY

Golf

As we went walking after our tee shots, I asked Dafydd how and when he thought golf got started. His answer amused me. "It seems the birth of golf and the evolution of whisky occurred at about the same time in history, and they have been inseparable ever since."

By the time we entered the fairway he had explained to me that in 1457, King James II banned not only golf but also soccer, as he felt these sports were distracting his militias from practicing archery. Archery was essential for the nation's defense, and therefore this ban was strictly enforced and lasted for another hundred years.

"Then at last, there was golf for the masses. Lads like you and me." He said with a smile as he pulled a midiron from his bag.

As we played on, he continued with his stories.

Whisky

Dafydd explained that the precise origin of Scotland's popular distilled liquor was not known, but that the distilling process is thought to have originated somewhere in Asia. There, it was first used in the production of perfume. As this distillation process moved around the world, some people, by applying red grapes during the process, found it then produced a red wine, or, if they applied white grapes, it then made a white wine. When this distilling process at last made its way to Scotland, a land and climate not known for great grape harvests, the Scots instead substituted different types of grains. This process resulted in a clear, golden-colored "wine." This new "wine" was formally labeled Usige Beath—or the "water of life."

Looking up and behind me, Dafydd saw an angry, blackened sky and a storm that was fast approaching. His voice got louder as he continued, "And for one glorious moment in the history of mankind, the rich and the poor had some things in common: golf and whisky. The one was the creator of the great thirst! The other, the quencher of that thirst," he said, now nearly yelling as the wind and rains began to batter the course and sent us running.

The Sand Dune

Pulling our golf clubs in with us, we crouched low and crawled under the lip of the sand dune we had chosen for shelter. Huddled together under a canopy of wildly waving sea grass, we watched the sheets of teeming rain blow across the fairway where we had left our balls. The storm's strong winds had even forced the sea gulls to leave the sky and seek shelter.

While catching his breath, Dafydd passed his flask of whisky to me. He watched me grimace as I swallowed the fiery liquid, and with a knowing smile he supported my effort, saying, "If they hadn't invented golf, we never would have needed the damned whisky."

Taking the flask back, he continued, "You know, whisky was first thought to be a brown table wine; a bottle of red, a bottle of white, and a bottle of brown. They were the accepted accompaniment to a meal, and it was considered good manners by all classes of society to offer all three at mealtime."

Dafydd took another swig from the flask as we sat there, amply sheltered, waiting for the gale to pass. "There were, and still are, people that think whisky has magical medicinal properties. For them it seemed a remedy for most common aches and pains, the preservation of good health, and the prolonging of life. Some used it to ease the depressions brought on by poverty and war."

He again offered the flask to me, but I waved it off, allowing him the honor of finishing the drink. "This beautiful caramel-colored 'water of life' escorted many hearty souls from cradle to grave. A mother's milk! A miracle in a glass! A gift for us all, from God!" he said with a big smile, lifting the flask up as if to toast.

Before It Was Called Golf

The fast-moving squall had now passed us, leaving behind a bright, breezy afternoon in its wake. The sea air was fresh, the gulls were again soaring in the bright sunlight, and the rest of the day looked favorable for golf. I watched Dafydd awkwardly stand up and hastily begin to brush the sand from his clothes saying, "This game will make even a wealthy man act like a commoner...hiding from the rain...crawling around in a dirty sand dune. What a mess!" he angrily mumbled to himself.

He turned away from me and went stomping off toward the sand dunes, saying, "Come with me, lad." I quickly followed after him, leaving our clubs behind and our balls lying out in the fairway.

"Forget all that," he growled with a disgusted wave back at the beautifully cared-for course we had been playing. "Let me show you where and how the game of golf got started."

Dafydd was talking about a game that was played before it was called "golf."

"Remember, lad, they used a stick of driftwood and sea shells; not bloody clubs and balls like us!"

We skirted the wet grasses that hung over the path he had chosen for us to climb. When we reached the top of a sandy hill, we found before us a cathedral of beautiful rolling dunes overflowing with wildlife, yellow flowering gorse, lilac heather, and green tufted seagrasses.

"The unspoiled coastal area between the sea and the fertile soils that surround Scotland are correctly known as wastelands," Dafydd continued. "Often barren, these sandy lands are home only to the native sea grasses and strong-rooted bushes that can withstand the harsh weather and winds that buffet these beach fronts. These areas are properly known as the *links-land*; or the useless land that links the two food sources, the one food source being the sea, the other being the arable fertile soils."

There was great timing to his story as he led me through the very places he spoke of.

"Ingeniously, somewhere in the mists of Scotland's past, there came an idea that allowed for a proper use of this *links-land*. It may not have been any one person's idea, but instead many people, searching for a creative and fun way to avoid boredom."

The Rabbits

Dafydd stepped off and to the side of the path and pointed at a hole in the ground. "This is a *form*, a shallow hole dug by rabbits. The underground network of tunnels connecting these forms is called a *warren*. The rabbits dig many forms throughout the dunes and they use them to escape from predators. Rabbits are nocturnal by nature, so these forms go unused during most of the day."

Then, looking out towards the distant green-blue sea, he waved his arm across the vast expanse of sand and grass adding, "Rabbits will construct their warrens in the hardiest grassy areas throughout the sandy dunes. It's the strong roots of this grass that hold the sand firm above their tunnels. They stamp their big hind legs and feet to flatten the sand and soil until it became firm enough to protect their warren from collapse. These flattened platforms became the targets we today call putting greens."

The Fair Way

We carefully worked our way through the weather-worn paths that took us between the spiny gorse, whins, brooms, and wild grasses that fortified these dunes. Dafydd pointed out various possible platforms that now lay hidden and unused.

"These early golfers would find sticks of driftwood lying about, and they would collect wee round sea shells called cockles from the beach. Cockles are inherently small and usually heart shaped; you know, 'the cockles of your heart'?"

He looked at me. I listened.

"They found that cockles were easier to hit than was a clam, a mussel, or a snail. Clam shells are disc shaped and broader. They say that all cockles are clams, but not all clams are cockles. Anyway, cockles became these early golfers shell of choice." I just nodded my head allowing him to ramble.

After a while, he stopped talking and a quiet calm settled over us. We stood there side by side, looking out at an undefined horizon, hidden now by a soft melding of the sea and sky.

Then he continued, "They'd hit these shells onto these platforms and then into the forms. Then they would retrieve the shell, choose another platform somewhere else in the dunes, and hit to that one. They created common pathways leading from platform to platform, and soon that became an agreed-upon routing. Eventually these pathways were named 'fairways,' as they became the 'fairer way' for them to hit their cockle shells."

We began walking again. He explained that after frequent retrievals of these cockle shells, the forms would weaken and eventually cave in. "They needed to be shored up, but no one knew what size to make the holes."

The Monkey Trap

We stopped again, this time near a ground hugging, fragrant patch of lilac heather.

"Monkeys are shy. When they see you approach, they will hide. A sure way to lure a monkey out into the open is to place a fig or another sweet fruit into a small knothole in a tree."

Dafydd was looking at me to make sure I was listening.

"Once he sees you leave, the monkey will seek out the fruit you left. Reaching into the knot hole, he will grasp the fruit, and by making a fist he finds that he can't pull his hand back out, but he won't let go of the bloody fruit. So now he is caught. He caught himself, the damned fool."

I could see where Dafydd was taking me. The size of the cup used to shore up the hole would need to be large enough to allow the average man's clenched hand to be removed while holding a cockle, or a ball.

Looking around, I noticed a small rabbit hole underneath the branches of a wide thicket of yellow gorse. I walked over to have a look at that hole, and I wondered to myself just what size cup I would have suggested. When I turned back to Dafydd with my thoughts, I saw him standing there with his mouth open and his tongue extended, squinting up at his flask with one eye closed, furiously shaking it in hopes that he could somehow produce one more drop of whisky.

The Jewels

As we slowly walked back to the course, I sensed that Dafydd had something else that he wanted me to know.

"That is how I see it," he said. "There is no other game, anywhere, that can compare. I mean, what other game would allow an obscure player to be the sole referee of his own actions? In other words, to give a personal accounting of his efforts when out of sight, and full well expect the other players to believe him! It is truly an extraordinary game!"

Memories

I'm back home now. My golf that day has long been forgotten—but not my time and talk with Dafydd under that sand dune. Nor have I forgotten the things we talked about as we roamed those bucolic rolling dunes of sand, all dappled with yellow, green and lavender flora.

I will go back there, someday.

And I'll search through those dunes until I find a stick of driftwood and a little round sea shell.

Then I'll play that game.

The game that was played before it was called golf.

REAL GOLF

I have found that the farther I can get from the obvious trophy courses when I play, the more authentic my golfing experiences are. These "remote masterpieces" that I have enjoyed are considered by some to be the lesser courses. Yet for me they have been sources of much pleasure. First, we should make note that the game of golf began on useless sandy soils and near the sea.

Golf

Thankfully, golf is not played on a standardized playing surface. Providing you have a hole, a teeing ground, a club, and a ball, golf can be played anywhere! A golf course can consist of nine or eighteen holes. That does not mean that there can't be twelve or six.

I once played a course somewhere in the Caribbean where there was but one small putting green, and encircling it were six teeing areas. We played "paradise rules," allowing us free drops from the random coconuts and other fronds of bracken we found scattered throughout the sandy, unkempt playing area. Our golfing struggles became such good fun we went around three times!

Executive Golf

The "executive course" differs from the standard course in that the majority of holes are par-3, with maybe some par-4 holes. These shorter-length layouts are intended for beginners, older golfers, and those who lack the time or desire to play on a standard-length, pricey course.

Championship Golf

One evening I played a fun match with my mates along a beach in Scotland, right in between a famous championship golf course and the sea. We placed a bottle of malt whisky on the sand to act as both our tee marker and as a locater of the hole that we had just dug.

Away we played—one club only—hitting full shots, until we reached "the sand dune with a red slatted fence above it." Then we turned around to hit our shots back to the hole we had dug.

Our championship's format?

He with the fewest shots won the bottle of whisky.

Our only rule? The winner shares all!

This is real golf, and it was fun!

THAT LITTLE STONE BRIDGE

"Pint o' bitter, is it, love?" She seemed to be reading my mind.

It had been a spirited morning walk and we had built up quite the thirst. This was our first day at St. Andrews. The same St. Andrews with the Old Course that plays out from, loops around itself, and then returns to the center of the medieval town that is the home of golf. Both the first and final holes lie so innocently in front of the old grey building where the rules of the game have always been discussed, argued, and enacted.

"Thanks. I think we'll each have a pint of bitter, Molly." I had just read her name tag, neatly pinned to the front of her starched white blouse. Molly, just bumping into middle age, has kept herself well.

"Aye. Sit there and relax. It will take just a moment to draw. You'll find it is well worth the wait."

We settled ourselves into our seats.

There is beauty walking into a pub and having the barkeep simply pull you a pint of the house favorite. No lists. No decisions. She just slings you a drink. She knows what you would like.

The Swilken Burn

The Swilken Burn, that romantic little waterway that meanders across the first and eighteenth fairways. There it sits, with its companion, "that little stone bridge," that will today help you, as it has so many others, to cross over the burn. First, the tee shots. Then the photo. Nowhere is the presence of the game's past ghosts more apparent than when you are standing on "that little stone bridge." It's haunting. Your foursome will, from this day forth, always be standing on those hallowed stones where all the greats have stood. Then off you will scurry, somehow happier, to complete that final hole.

The Valley of Sin

Golf was never meant to be fair. It is meant more to be a revealer of one's character. And nowhere will you reveal more of your golf self than with the tricky terrain you are now facing called the Valley of Sin. Leaning over the fence to watch how you elect to play through that swale in front of that final green are the local citizens. The pitch and run? A high wedge shot? Maybe you will find comfort in a long putt. They all can be risky. They all have ruined good scores. But try not to think about it. These townspeople will applaud your every effort.

Cheers

"There you are, lads. To your health!" Molly said. There, in front of the four of us, sat three pints o' bitter. We all sat there in silence, not wanting to be the one to question this friendly lass, but where was the fourth pint?

Finally, our fourth spoke up.

"Excuse me? I would like a pint, too," said he.

"O'? You still have your cap on. I thought you were leaving," replied she. Embarrassed . . . the cap was quickly removed.

"Pint o' bitter it is, love," replied she . . . standing there . . . with one eyebrow raised . . . in her starched white blouse.

CLASSIC GOLF

There is much expressed frustration about golf's waning popularity. I like to think that it is the sport preserving itself—or that maybe golf is in the midst of a renaissance.

There's always been a perceived elitism that surrounds the game of golf. Recently, that seems to be changing with the traditional hierarchy that once ran the clubs being replaced by more democratic forms of governing.

Until recently, most attempts made to promote golf have been focused on the professional side of the game. Discussions about golf, in the public's eyes, were always about pro golfers, their new equipment, and their most recent achievements. Rarely was the importance of amateur golf and the *everyday golfer* heralded.

Everyday Golfers

Everyday golfers genuinely like golf. They like it because they enjoy playing the game and it is their enjoyment that powers the sport forward. It's not because of the pros. Not because of television. Not because of the media attention. It is the enjoyment of these *everyday golfers* that will determine the future of golf.

Golf Preserving Itself

With all the technological and agronomic improvements, golf has not become more attractive. Golf, instead, has become quite costly, too difficult, and rudely time consuming.

The game was never meant to be played in a sterile stadium of man-made gardens, waterways and walking paths. It was born on rugged, wind-swept land where you could feel nature surrounding you on every hole, in every hazard, and during every swing.

This "golf land" was for us to share with the burrowing animals, the worm castings, and animal dung. It offered us an opportunity to experience the changing weather. Not just the clouds and sunshine, but also the wind and the rain. It provided us with an opportunity to appreciate the parts of life we usually avoid.

Classic Golf

There is a difference between modern golf and *classic golf*. Modern golf is like playing through a green house. *Classic golf* is like playing through a garden.

Classic golf courses, the ones that nature routed for us through the land-scape or seaside sands, are rare and exist in places often difficult to find. This type of golf course, the one that required little or no help from man when it was built, evolves slowly. Unfortunately, we don't always allow the time for that to occur.

The Renaissance

Here are some uplifting, interesting thoughts, concerning a return to *classic golf*.

The Course—You can tee off from wherever you like.

(Make the course as long or short as you wish.)

The Clubhouse—A shelter from bad weather.

(No need for high-back leather chairs.)

The Golf Shop—A small room supplying your golfing needs.

(Balls, tees, scorecards.)

The Grill Room—Get your own drink and sandwich from the fridge.

(If you would like a home-cooked meal, go home.)

The Locker Room—A room with a few benches and hooks on the walls.

(The hot-water showers are at home, along with the home-cooked meals.)

The Rules—No rules.

(If you have to ask, you can't)

Classic golf.

Now doesn't that sound like fun.

THE FIRST WOMEN GOLFERS

Mary, Queen of Scots, may have been the first woman to find golf worthy of her time. When she played golf, she would have her cadets accompany her, some to carry her clubs and some for her protection, as the links courses the Queen played led her away from the safety of her castle.

The Ladies' Golf Club

In the nineteenth century, croquet and archery were the accepted female sports. Then, in 1867, the Ladies' Golf Club of St. Andrews was formed, ironically, by the male members of the "men-only" Royal and Ancient Golf Club. They were offering a golfing opportunity to their women, and the women relished that opportunity.

Ladies' Putting Club

In 1948, the Ladies' Golf Club changed its name to the Ladies' Putting Club. It was "considered unacceptable for women to take the club back past their shoulder," so by forming the Ladies' Putting Club, the women could play the game and comfortably fit in with the times. When they putted, the women golfers would dress up, wearing their fancy long skirts, lacy blouses, and wide-brim hats.

The function of this club was to oversee and operate the Himalayas, the fascinating eighteen-hole putting course located alongside the Old Course at St. Andrews. Initially the course was to be used just by the women members, but in time, the rules were altered and another class of membership was added. That membership was called the "gentleman associate."

The Himalayas

The Himalayas putting course extends over about two acres of rolling terrain. The holes are about 10 to 20 yards in length. There is a section with ankle-deep rough, there is a water hazard, and there is out of bounds. The humps and hills that you must putt over are often five or six feet high. These obstacles are tricky and make it hard to calculate just where the ball may roll. The speed with which you putt the ball is critical, because the ball needs to gently slide off of those hills and into the valleys, stopping near the cup. There may be occasions when you will need to hit your ball a few yards past the cup and up a hill, where it will then reverse and come back down that slope, hopefully stopping by the cup.

The Himalayas putting course is only open for half of the year and plays host to some sixty-thousand players annually.

The putting course typically takes less than an hour to putt around, with the lowest recorded score for the eighteen holes being 34: three 1s, one 3, and the rest 2s.

The holes are changed twice each week.

It typically takes one man seven hours to mow; the steepest hillocks are mown by hand, while the flatter portions are maintained using a power mower.

Tradition

Each year, the president of the Ladies' Putting Club and captain of the R&A play a match on the Himalayas. The match is played precisely at 3:30 p.m. on a Tuesday afternoon, and it is "etched in stone," meaning the match is played regardless of "cranky weather."

The ladies can use any putter they choose, while the R&A men must use "long-snooted putters with hickory shafts." When the match is completed, refreshments are served, proper speeches made, and a trophy presented to the winner.

Home of Golf

Citizens of St. Andrews care deeply about golf. They feel both a responsibility to preserve the game's history, etiquette, and traditions and an obligation to transfer their love and knowledge of this game to the younger generations.

The Himalayas offer a taste of golf that anyone can experience in a light-hearted spirit.

And it should appease even the most traditional of players to know that he or she will be putting on real links turf.

Just like the turf Mary, Queen of Scots, first learned to putt on.

MARION HOLLINS—THE WOMEN'S NATIONAL CLUB

Marion Hollins, a wealthy American amateur golfer, was the first female golf course developer. She helped create the Women's National Golf and Tennis Club, Cypress Point Club, and Pasatiempo Golf Club. Marion was also the ultimate reason Bobby Jones hired Dr. Alister MacKenzie to design Augusta National Golf Course.

The Women's National Golf and Tennis Club, Glen Head, Long Island—1923

Hollins was instrumental in starting the Women's National, a club that was owned, financed, and managed entirely by women. Male golfers were not permitted to be members, but they could play the course as guests.

Oddly enough, the Augusta National Golf Course, a "men-only" club, was forming at the same time. Much to everyone's amusement, it was rumored that the Women's National Club was attracting new members more readily than Augusta.

The uncertainty brought on by the Great Depression and the Second World War weakened this unique club and, after successfully operating for eighteen years, it was forced to close.

Cypress Point, Monterey, California—1926

Cypress Point would become Hollins's second golf course project. The developer of the Monterey Peninsula was Samuel F. B. Morse (a.k.a. the Duke of Del Monte). Morse and Hollins together fashioned a first-class private golf club on Cypress Point. Hollins hired the famed golf course architect Dr. Alister MacKenzie, who there created what many believe to be the greatest golf course in the world.

Dr. MacKenzie humbly gave his friend Marion full credit for the design of the world-famous par-3 sixteenth hole.

"To give honor where it is due," MacKenzie wrote in *The Spirit of St. Andrews*, "I must say that, except for minor details in construction, I was in no way responsible for the famous sixteenth hole. It was largely due to the vision of Miss Marion Hollins, the founder of Cypress Point. It was suggested to her by the late Seth Raynor that it was a pity the carry over the ocean was too long to enable a hole to be designed on this particular site. Miss Hollins said she did not think it was an impossible carry. She then teed up a ball and drove to the middle of the site for the suggested green."

Pasatiempo Golf Club, Santa Cruz, California—1929

It was also Hollins's vision that gave birth to the Pasatiempo Golf Club in Santa Cruz, California. She again recruited Dr. Alister MacKenzie for the course design. They successfully opened the course with an exhibition match featuring both Hollins and Bobby Jones, along with Glenna Collett Vare and Cyril Tolley, the great British amateur. The Pasatiempo Club quickly became a fashionable playground for the rich and famous, hosting both Hollywood stars and East Coast socialites.

It was Hollins's enthusiasm about the Pasatiempo course design during that match that persuaded Bobby Jones to hire Dr. MacKenzie as the architect of his Augusta National Golf Club.

Augusta National, Augusta, Georgia—1933

The Augusta club was struggling with its finances, and its chairman, Clifford Roberts, didn't have the money he owed MacKenzie. Dr. MacKenzie wanted Marion—his wealthy associate—to do a site inspection of the important project. He wrote to the Augusta Club of Marion:

"She has been associated with me in three golf courses and not only are her own ideas valuable, but she is thoroughly conversant in regard to the character of work I like. I want her views and her personal impressions regarding the way the work is being carried out." Clifford Roberts still objected to MacKenzie sending Marion (a woman). MacKenzie continued: "I do not know of any man who has sounder ideas."

Hollins did make the trip, and MacKenzie later wrote that, "She was most favorably impressed with it." The Augusta National Golf Course design was completed by Dr. Alister MacKenzie and formally opened in 1933.

Ms. Marion Hollins died quietly at fifty-one years of age, during World War II, while the world was looking elsewhere.

USGA HONORS MICKEY WRIGHT 2012

Mickey Wright is a living legend in the world of golf. She was the premier ladies golfer in the 1960s, winning eighty-two times, and she is ranked as the ninth greatest golfer of all time. There is no golfer, man or woman, who has dominated an era the way Mickey Wright did hers.

1963 Season

At just twenty-eight years of age, Wright won thirteen tournaments in a single season. It is a record that still stands today.

After the 1963 season ended, LPGA golfing great Kathy Whitworth recalled, "I was feeling really good about myself. I had won eight tournaments. Even though Mickey had won thirteen, it was still the best year I'd ever had."

After a momentary pause, she added, "Then someone asked me right at the beginning of 1964: 'How did you do last year?' It made me feel like quitting."

Mickey Wright won four USGA Women's Opens before she was thirty years of age.

Mickey is the only player to win four LPGA Championships.

Mickey is the only female player to have held four major championship titles at the same time.

Mickey twice shot 62, bettering that era's scoring record by two strokes.

No Mickey–No Tourney

In the early days of the LPGA, if women's tournament golf was ever discussed, it was in an offhand way. If the girls played well enough one week, they might make enough prize money to get them to the next event. It was also not unusual for the tournament sponsors to threaten canceling their tournaments if Mickey didn't play. The success of the ladies tour and the livelihoods of her fellow pros were becoming her responsibility.

Lenny Wirtz, then the LPGA's tournament director, revealed that, "No other golfer did more to contribute to the growth of the LPGA. We were struggling to find thirty girls to play the tour because we weren't paying enough money to the lower spots," explained Wirtz. "I said to Mickey, 'I want to reduce the winner's percentage of the purse from 20 to 15 percent of the pot so we can pay more to the others.' The only player it was going to affect was Mickey, because she was winning everything."

Mickey's response?

"If it's going to help the tour, I'm for it."

Wright Retired at Age Thirty-four

Kathy Whitworth reflected, "I had been shooting at the top for years, and suddenly the top is gone. Even if I do turn out to be number one, it won't taste the same. Everybody is going to say, 'Mickey Wright wasn't playing.'"

Whitworth, who has since recorded eighty-eight tournament wins (more than any other golfer in history), said, "We could all see she was just so far superior to anyone else. People don't remember just how good she was."

When he was asked to discuss her golf swing, golfing great and swing aficionado Ben Hogan simply stated, "She had the finest golf swing I ever saw."

The Mickey Wright Room

The United States Golf Association Museum in Far Hills, New Jersey, has accepted and will display a collection of more than two hundred of Wrights personal artifacts. The collection will be displayed in the Mickey Wright Room. Wright is only the fourth player—and first woman—to have a gallery in her name at the museum.

Thanks, Mickey.

We are honored.

John J. McDermott, Jr

The short, gutsy career of Johnny McDermott and the effect he had on golf's early development in this country has faded with time and is sadly unknown to most. His career was derailed by mental illness and he is rarely discussed or acknowledged today except by historians. As a young professional at the Atlantic City Country Club, in New Jersey, Johnny would practice his game before and after work, often in darkness. He would place newspapers on the ground at various distances for his targets, and listen to hear if his shots were landing accurately.

Career Highlights

It seemed that with every success McDermott achieved, a bigger failure would follow.

In 1911, at the Chicago Golf Club, in Illinois, he became the first American born pro to win the U.S. Open. The previous 16 championships had been won by players born in Britain.

In 1912 he won his second straight US Open championship at the CC of Buffalo, posting the lowest score ever for a 72 hole event.

Although it was McDermott's back-to-back victories in 1911 and 1912 that elevated interest in golf to new levels, it was Francis Ouimet's 1913 U.S. Open victory that received the most credit for the game's blossoming popularity in the United States.

McDermott's career peaked in 1913 at Shawnee-on-Delaware in Pennsylvania when he won the Shawnee Open. Having handily defeated

two prominent English pros, Harry Vardon and Ted Ray, McDermott jovi-
ally boasted of his own victory. His gloating was deemed offensive by the
press and his fellow players, and he was prompted to make an apology. The
public humiliation of having to apologize hurt him deeply.

In 1914 Transatlantic travel was difficult and delays common. McDermott,
met with various travel complications, arrived late and missed his starting
time in that year's British Open at Prestwick Golf Club in Scotland. The
tournament officials compassionately offered him a later tee time, but he
refused saying it would be unfair to the other players if they amended that
rule just for him.

On his early return to the United States, his passenger ship set sail in a heavy
mist and collided with a freighter in the English Channel. The ship's water
tight doors were secured and the lifeboats swung out but luckily they were
never lowered nor boarded. The ship limped its way back through the fog to
safer waters and at last returned to port. Though a harrowing experience for
all, the ship and its passengers had avoided disaster.

The stock market losses, the prompted apology and public humiliation at
Shawnee, and the near death experience on his return from Britain were
more than McDermott could handle. These misfortunes affected him greatly
and he suffered a mental breakdown. Now a broken man, he was committed
to the State Hospital in Norristown, Pennsylvania.

His Last Game

Golfers are a close knit group and have great respect for their champions.
Knowing of McDermott's prowess, the doctors at the Norristown Hospital
set up a makeshift six-hole course on the asylum grounds to perhaps help
him convalesce. When the great Walter Hagen came to visit, he and the
afflicted champion played some golf together on the little course.

Afterwards, as Hagen was leaving, McDermott eased his departure by saying, "I don't think I ever saw a more beautiful view than from here. Tell the boys I'm getting along just fine." Hagen made sure that all of Johnny's friends knew how he felt.

After an abbreviated but outstanding 5 year career, and nearly 80 years on earth, John J. McDermott, Jr., passed away. The simple inscription on his monument reads;

"First American Born Golf Champion 1911-1912"

SIR WALTER HAGEN

He was "Sir Walter." He was "The Haig." He was the most colorful character the game of golf will ever know. He alone brought class to a sport that once regarded those in the amateur sector as being above the professionals.

Walter Hagen was the first American professional golfer. He made his living only by playing the game. Hagen stayed at the best hotels, threw the best parties, and was sometimes driven right to the first tee in a limousine. "I never wanted to be a millionaire," he said with a big smile. "I just wanted to live like one."

Hagen was the first athlete to earn $1 million playing a sport.

Hagen was the first American to win the British Open.

Hagen was the first sportsman named to the list of Best Dressed Americans.

With these qualities so frequently mentioned, his supreme abilities as a player are sometimes wrongly overlooked.

"The Haig" had an erratic long game, though he was blessed with an uncanny ability to create spectacular recovery shots. His creativity befuddled even the best of his opponents. Walking from the green to the next tee, just loud enough for his opponent to hear, he would recall his shots saying, "Three of those, and one of them, still count four."

After he defeated Bob Jones, 12 and 11, in a seventy-two-hole challenge match in 1926, which was played to decide which of them was the greatest golfer of the day, even Jones couldn't contain his frustration. "When a man misses his drive, and then misses his second shot, and then wins the hole with a birdie," said Jones, "it gets my goat." Then, upon review of the day, he would say. "I love to play with Walter. He can come nearer beating luck itself than anybody I know."

"The Haig" also understood the effect playing competitive golf had on certain golfers. While preparing to spend a night out on the town on the eve of the final match for the 1926 PGA Championship (which he won), someone mentioned to Walter that his opponent was already in bed.

"Yes," responded Hagen, "but he isn't sleeping."

"Sir Walter," ever the gentlemen, was never known to criticize a golf course. Instead he would call them "sporty little layouts," or he would say, "that was the best course, of its kind, that I have ever played."

When he died in Traverse City, Michigan, on October 5, 1969, there was no doubt that he had lived his life well. His gestures had been grand, but he had always been wonderfully human. Hagen's kindly face and mannerisms invited rather than repelled the common man. He was a joy for average golfers to watch because they knew he genuinely enjoyed what he was doing.

Hagen once expressed his creed in these words: "You're only here for a short visit. Don't hurry. Don't worry. And don't forget to smell the flowers along the way."

"Sir Walter" Hagen. He was American golf.

GENE SARAZEN–THE SQUIRE

Born Eugenio Saracini, he later changed his name to Gene Sarazen thinking that it "sounded more like a golfer's name." Later, he was affectionately nicknamed "The Squire."

Gene Sarazen turned pro in 1920, while still a teenager. "Nobody gave me lessons," he said. "I used to watch the players in tournaments. My favorite was Walter Hagen. He was my hero."

Career Highlights

—At the age of 20, he burst onto the golf scene by winning three majors in 1922-23. His back-to-back victory in his 1923 PGA Championship title was achieved by defeating his idol, the legendary Walter Hagen.

—Sarazen is credited with inventing the first sand wedge in 1931.

—Using a tip about warming up from baseball immortal Ty Cobb, Sarazen developed a weighted practice club by filling the shaft of a club with buckshot. He is thought to have used it on his trans Atlantic trip to play in the 1932 British Open, where he led for all four rounds and won by five shots.

—He was the first golfer to win the professional career grand slam (Masters, U.S. Open, British Open, PGA Championship). Only four other players—Ben Hogan, Jack Nicklaus, and Gary Player, and Tiger Woods—have accomplished that feat.

—Sarazen owns one of the most remarkable records in PGA Championship history. He was not only the tournaments youngest champion (age 20), but he was also its oldest participant (age 70) when he played in the 1972 PGA Championship.

The Shot Heard Around The World

Sarazen stood on the par 5 fifteenth fairway during the final round of the 1935 Masters trailing Craig Wood by three strokes. Indicating that he was out of contention, his playing partner, Walter Hagen, in a loud voice hollered over to him, "Hurry up, will ya? I've got a date tonight!"

Sarazen sped things up dramatically by holing the shot for a double-eagle 2. It was this 4 wood shot that placed him in a 36 hole playoff that he brilliantly won the next day.

In an interview with The Augusta Chronicle in 1995, Sarazen—when asked about his double eagle and eventual win—comically responded saying, "If I hadn't won, it would have been a double eagle without feathers."

Grand Rivalries

Gene Sarazen, Walter Hagen, and amateur Bobby Jones, were the world's dominant players during the 1920s. The grand rivalries among these three great champions significantly expanded interest in golf as the United States became the dominant power in golf.

The competition between Hagen and Sarazen is considered one of the games greatest rivalries. In 1922, Hagen, the 30 year old British Open champion, and Sarazen, the 20 year old U.S.Open Champion, played a challenge match. The younger Sarazen won the match 3 up with 2 holes to play. As Sarazen would later explain: " I didn't like the way he kept calling me 'kid.' I was a champion and I wanted Hagen to respect me as a champion."

Story Book Ending

Sarazen, at the age of 71, celebrated the 50th anniversary of his first appearance in the British Open, by making his farewell appearance in the 1973 British Open at Royal Troon Golf Club in Ayrshire, Scotland. On the famed "Postage Stamp," a short but demanding par-3 at Royal Troon, Sarazen made a hole-in-one. His "ace" brought back joyous memories of his "shot heard around the world" made decades before at the Masters.

The following day, the television cameras curiously followed his play at the Postage Stamp when to everyone's delight he holed a bunker shot for a birdie two on the very same hole.

"The Squire." He left the game with the same flair he brought to it.

"CHAMPAGNE" TONY LEMA

Tony Lema was nicknamed "Champagne Tony" at the 1962 Orange County Open in California after promising the media that they would all drink champagne should he win that event. His storybook victory the next day launched Tony's career, and the champagne and money began flowing. "Champagne Tony" had become golf's media darling.

To Be or Not To Be

"First he is going and then he isn't," his wife, Betty, complained of Tony's indecisiveness to participate in the 1964 British Open, being held in St. Andrews, Scotland. "I don't know and, believe me, neither does he. Tell me, are other golfers like normal people?"

After completing the fourth round of the 1964 Whitemarsh Open in Philadelphia, Pennsylvania, "Champagne Tony" finally decided that he would play. With his decision now made, he could speak freely of his goals. "I want to win a major championship. It is on my schedule of things to do, and I am going to do it."

Most of the other pros had concluded that it would be fruitless for him or any golfer to play at Whitemarsh, travel to Scotland, and then expect to win the British Open the very next week. Especially playing a quirky seaside links course like St. Andrews, where first-time players are usually told not to think about scoring, just take in the experience and have fun.

Keen Sense of Beauty

Lema had just finished playing his few practice holes on the Old Course at St. Andrews when a reporter holding a microphone came up to him and asked, "What's your first impression of St. Andrews, Tony?"

Ever the diplomat, Lema said of the course, "I feel like I'm visiting an old grandmother. She's crotchety and eccentric but also elegant, and anyone who doesn't fall in love with her has no imagination."

Five days later, having played beautiful links-style golf over the tricky Old Course at St. Andrews, "Champagne Tony" won the coveted and historic Open Championship. Along with the Claret Jug came the warm admiration of the once-skeptical Scottish galleries and his fellow pros back home.

Sad Headlines

It was not long after his victory at St. Andrews that the delightful "Champagne Tony," whose quick wit and impish smile had charmed the golfing millions of two continents, died along with his wife, Betty, in a plane crash. Ironically, the plane crashed and burst into flames on the seventh hole of a golf course.

Lema the Legend

The legend of "Champagne Tony" Lema has now faded, but hopefully it will never be forgotten. His "swinging" lifestyle may seem roguish, brazen, or anachronistic in these more puritanical times, when drinking, smoking, and playboy behaviors are considered nutritionally and politically incorrect. But for those who were lucky enough to know him, his legend is unforgettable. For the short time he was with us, it was "Champagne Tony's" decision to give it his best shot.

Tony Lema made it known to us all that, "Life is not a practice round."

DOUG SANDERS—WHAT HE GAVE AWAY

Suppose you've spent a lifetime pursuing your childhood dream. Then, just as your efforts are to be rewarded, you fail. And you fail in front of the world. Would you ever want to relive that shattered dream? If not, that's what separates you from Doug Sanders. Sanders has come back to "the Auld Grey Toon" all seven times it has hosted the British Open since his fall.

Pro golfer and fashion icon Doug Sanders—he once owned 365 pairs of golf and dress shoes, to match his vast rainbow of a wardrobe—had the chance to live his dream at the 1970 British Open at St. Andrews. It is one of the saddest moments in golf.

The Gift

Doug admits he gave the tournament away.

"I missed a 30-inch putt on the last green that would have won the British Open. It's all anybody wants to talk about. What can I say? It's what I remember most, too."

His drive was center cut. Dressed in his matching magenta-colored clothing and shoes, he walked confidently up the home hole toward his victory. He paused to look the situation over, and then, uncharacteristically, he walked forward to the green. Some say the extra preparation merely played with his heartstrings and added tension to the moment.

His approach ended some thirty-five feet past the flag.

His approach putt finished three feet from the hole.

Wind-blown Memories

Standing over the short putt, Sanders started to take his backstroke when he abruptly stopped. A speck of dirt—or maybe a childhood memory—had blown into his line.

"I didn't have my own shoes until I was about ten or eleven years old," he said. "Had hand-me-downs—two lefts, two rights. I'd cut the toes out and put tape on 'em."

Stepping out with his expensive, magenta-colored left shoe while keeping the right one in place, he leaned over and brushed the speck aside.

One day he had won a bet and finally had enough cash for a new pair of shoes. "If I ever strutted," he said, "that was probably the biggest strut I ever had. That was one of the most proud moments of my life—I had my own shoes."

When Sanders replaced his left shoe in his stance, he noticed that he had placed it in a different spot.

From the instant he putted the ball, he wanted to pull it back. It missed by about an inch.

A Place to Cry

Sanders, his wife Scotty, and singer Buddy Greco had rented a farmhouse in the outskirts of the town. That night, Sanders went out alone to walk among the cows in the pasture in the late evening dusk. He lay down in the meadow, looked up at the grey sky, and let go of some old childhood dreams. His tears came to comfort him.

"It was hard. I could do anything and never let it bother me emotionally. Like when my father was dying, I didn't show anything. If he died, he died. I loved him."

Then he revealed. "My brother, Ernest, was blind from age four. He picked up a dynamite cap in a coal yard and lit it with a splinter. Blew his fingers off and his eyes out."

Doug had led his blind brother, Ernest, into their father's room the night he died. "Of course, Ernest had to run his hands over the old man's face to see him."

He paused, "I went to a place I had in the backyard—I always had a place in the backyard to cry."

Many Years Gone By

"You know, time moves on, and you get forgotten. That's all right. I'm at the stage where all that matters is giving back," explained Mr. Sanders.

"When you die, the only things you get to keep are what you gave away."

SANDY LYLE—
THE CHAMPIONS DINNER

Every year at the Masters, there is a Champions Dinner. The winner of the previous year's tournament selects the main course. The year that Scottish pro golfer Sandy Lyle made the selection, he chose haggis. This created quite a stir among the past champions, as haggis is made from the lungs, livers, and hearts—or, better said, from the leftover, otherwise-thrown-away parts—of sheep. When questioned about his choice, Sandy endorsed his selection saying, "I've enjoyed haggis at our clan gathering in the Highlands of Scotland, piped in by a piper, as required, and can vouch for it being one of the tastiest dishes ever."

The Celebration of the Haggis

Every January 25, Scottish poet Robert Burns' life and poetry are celebrated with a Burns Supper, featuring a main course of haggis. The evening's events are as follows.

Once all the invited guests are seated, the "Selkirk Grace" is orated.

> Some have meat and cannot eat,
> Some cannot eat that want it;
> But we have meat and we can eat,
> So let the Lord be thank it.

Then everyone stands and into the dining hall marches a piper, bagpipes loudly blaring. This gets everyone's attention, as you certainly cannot ignore the stirring sounds made by a bagpipe. If you have never heard bagpipes, this quote from Alfred Hitchcock may help to explain the sound:

"I understand the inventor of the bagpipes was inspired when he saw a man carrying an indignant, asthmatic pig under his arm. Unfortunately, the man-made object never equalled the purity of sound achieved by the pig."

Following the piper straight to the head table is the chef, who is carrying a large dish upon which lies a boiled haggis.

What Is Haggis?

After my first Burns Supper, I sat sharing the warmth of a smoky peat fire with that evening's piper, and I asked him to tell me all he knew about haggis. He said, "There is a small, hairy animal native only to the Scottish Highlands. It is called a haggis."

He paused to look around the room. Once our privacy was confirmed, he continued.

"There are two varieties of haggis. One is the female, who has the longer left legs. The other is the male, who has the longer right legs. The female can only run clockwise around a mountainside, while the male can only run counterclockwise."

He nipped at his whisky.

I nipped at mine.

"The two coexist peacefully, possibly because they are unable to propagate. When the male tries to mount his intended mate, he must turn to face in the same direction as she, but then, sadly, he loses his balance and tips over."

There I sat, tight lipped, ready to burst into laughter, as he slowly leaned in close to me and whispered, "Lad, you know that haggis, when excited, make a sound similar to that of a bagpipe. During the mating season, all the Highlands sound like a Scottish marching band is coming through."

Our Evening Draws Nigh

So now our whisky was gone; the peat fire dim. It was time for us to go.

Maybe it was the whisky, or maybe it was just me, but as I watched my friend the piper leave, I swore he was limping a bit to his left . . . and walking in a counterclockwise direction!

I thought to myself how lucky I had been. For now I too had enjoyed haggis in the Highlands of Scotland, just like Sandy Lyle.

THE HYNDMANS—SIMPLE ADVICE

William Hyndman III, 1915–2001

The Waynesborough Country Club course was wet after a night of heavy rain, and it was going to play long. I was paired with the best amateur golfer in the Philadelphia area, William Hyndman III. My plan that day was to play as well as I could and try not to make any foolish mistakes.

We had both hit long drives right down the first fairway. I walked up to my ball to check my yardage and lie, and after I looked things over, I found that I was standing ahead of where I should have been. Rather than make any sudden movement to correct my position, I thought it best just to stand still, figuring that Mr. Hyndman would tell me if he felt I was in his way. He set up to his ball, took his swing, and in a flash his ball flew right over my head and into the rough some 30 yards to the right of the green. It was a perfect shank!

His shot startled me. I was not sure what I should say or do, so I just went ahead with my shot, hitting my ball 15 feet short of the pin. After a brief search for his ball, he proceeded to hit his wedge shot close to the hole and made his par. It was as though it had been his plan all along. Perfect drive. Perfect shank. Perfect wedge. Perfect putt. On to the next hole.

While I was rethinking his play of the hole, I failed to notice some casual water between my ball and the cup, and that mistake caused me to three putt, making a bogey. Walking to the next tee, he mentioned to me that the rules provided relief from casual water. I was so embarrassed by my faux pas that I couldn't think of a sensible retort.

Our scores were close after we finished our morning round at Waynesborough, and we were still close after the first nine at Aronimink Golf Club. On the tenth hole, I hit two big hooks out of play. Mr. Hyndman went on to win that Patterson Cup; his score included that perfect shank.

He took me aside when we finished play and told me that I had been straightening my right leg on my backswing, and that was the cause of the two hooked tee shots. I was flattered that he had even noticed my swing, and I thanked him for taking the time to help me.

That is what I remember of William Hyndman III Paterson Cup victory in 1969.

William Hyndman IV, 1940–2012

William "Buck" Hyndman IV, though an accomplished amateur golfer, insurance executive, and car collector, was better known by the golfing community and all that knew him for being a constant and complete gentlemen.

A few seasons ago, he was driving the ball poorly and he asked me to help him with his swing. He told me he could not stop hitting wild hooks with his driver and asked if I could check him out.

"Buck," an accomplished amateur golfer, had won the club championship and the Crump Memorial Cup at Pine Valley Golf Club, was ten times the club champion at Huntington Valley Country Club, and had participated in eight USGA Amateur Championships. He was a special golfer who had been guided by many teachers, but none as impressive as his father, William Hyndman III. Buck told me he was looking for something simple to think of. Something like the advice his father used to give him.

As I watched him swing, I couldn't help but notice that he was straightening his right leg at the top of his backswing, just as I had in the 1969 Patterson Cup.

The advice I shared with Buck that day worked. It was simple advice.

Just like the advice his dad had shared with me some forty years before.

I was very fortunate to have known them both.

DAN JENKINS

I guess you just had to be there, and it's lucky for us that Dan Jenkins was. For sixty or so years he has written stories, humorously, about golf, a sport which at times can be taken a little too seriously.

On May 7, 2012, eighty-five-year-old writer Dan Jenkins was inducted into the World Golf Hall of Fame. He is the third writer in the Hall; the other two are regarded more as literary artists—Bernard Darwin and Herbert Warren Wind. That's fine with Jenkins. He prefers to interject humor.

Jenkins has been referred to as both "the quintessential *Sports Illustrated* writer" and "the best sportswriter in America." He has written more than five hundred articles for *Sports Illustrated* and is the author of eleven novels, including *The Dogged Victims of Inexorable Fate*, *Dead Solid Perfect*, and *The Glory Game at Goat Hills*.

Jenkins covered his first Masters in 1951, and the 2012 US Open at the Olympic Club was his 212th major tournament. What he claims to miss the most about those early days is the easy access to the players. He enjoyed walking the fairways with the pros back then and listening to what they had to say. The locker-room interviews and the friendly dinners that followed have "all been lost," he said.

America's Guest

George Low was one of the early journeymen of the sport, and one of the great characters in golf. As Dan Jenkins described him in his book *The Dogged Victims of Inexorable Fate*, "He is, all at once, America's guest, underground comedian, consultant, inventor of the overlapping grip for a beer can, and, more important, a man who has conquered the two hardest things in life—how to putt better than anyone ever, and how to live lavishly without an income."

Everybody Listened

Along the way someone nicknamed George Low "America's Guest," and that could not have been more accurate. It became his title. And that was all right with George. He never went anywhere unless he knew that there was someone with him that would pay his way.

There is a wonderful story about Low and Frank Stranahan of the Champion Spark Plug family. Frank hired George to drive his car from one tournament town to another, a common practice for the wealthier pros in those days. Then, Frank planned to fly to the next venue and meet George there to pick up his car.

Stranahan, attempting to retrieve his auto from George at the next town, found that his car never made it. Asking just where his car was, George told him, "You lost it in a crap game. The other guy made the hard eight."

It was Low's savant-like skills with a putter, his acceptance by the rich and famous, and a talent to insert an insult within joke that made him so welcome around the PGA Tour.

Most pros, superstitiously, never mention their putting, especially if they are on a hot streak. Low would always be bragging; and then he would badger you until you would give in and join him on the putting green. There you would personally experience his putting stroke; the stroke that took him anywhere he ever wanted to go. It was beautiful.

Everyone wanted to know, just what was his secret?

"Just tap it," he'd softly say with a wry grin.

And everybody listened.

THE GAME IS BIGGER THAN US ALL

GOLF: An ineffectual endeavor to put an insignificant pellet into an obscure hole with inadequate tools. Sir Winston Churchill.

It would seem to me that a sense of humor and a few more smiles would be a help for those of us who are trying to play the very complex game Sir Winston has so eloquently described.

Golf–2012

Sergio Garcia, after winning two golf tournaments, made a splash in Thailand when after a poor tee shot he threw his club into a nearby lake. This current bad boy of golf had recently been assessed the largest fine ever imposed on a player by the European Tour for his continued displays of rudeness.

John Daily walked off a golf course in Australia, after losing all his golf balls in a lake. It is reported that he will not be invited to play in their events again because of his continued displays of rudeness.

But this anger stuff is not new.

Golf–1950s

One of golf's most gifted players in the fifties, Tommy Bolt, also displayed a temper that overshadowed his career and tournament successes. His reputation for throwing both tantrums and his golf clubs brought with it reprimands, fines, and suspensions, along with the nickname of "Terrible Tempered Tommy."

There is one story that describes how Bolt, when standing in the last fairway viewing his shot, asked his caddy to recommend a club to hit. In response, his caddie suggested a 2-iron. Bolt snickered and said, "Are you kidding, son...the shot is only 100 or so yards long?" To which his caddy replied, "Mr. Bolt, that's the only club we have left in the bag."

"Terrible Tommy," when quizzed later about his antics, responded with a smile. "Here's irony for you: the driver goes the shortest distance when you throw it; and the putter flies farthest, followed then by the sand wedge."

Golf–1940s

Then there was the wondrously named Ky Laffoon back in the forties, whose playing career is decorated with storie's about his fits of anger brought on by his poor putting. During one frustrating round and after missing a short putt, Ky stood still by the hole glaring down at his putter. Suddenly, leaving the other players in his group standing there, he stormed off and went directly to the green side pond where he knelt down and held his putter under the water while shouting: "Drown, you son-of-a-b—, drown!"

When asked if it was true that he had just driven 400 miles to the next tournament site with his putter tied to the rear bumper of his car he calmly replied, "Just wanted to teach it a lesson."

It is a shame there are not more characters like Terrible Tommy and Ky around. They brought some fun and color into a game that can at times be taken all too seriously.

And I, for one, think that there is a Santa Claus . . . and I also hope that these stories are true.

BEN HOGAN'S ALLEY

Hogan Must Qualify

The year was 1953. Ben Hogan had just won the Masters at Augusta Golf Club, in Augusta, Georgia by five strokes and the U.S. Open at Oakmont in Pittsburgh, Pennsylvania by six. He now needed to win the British Open at Carnoustie Golf Course in Scotland to be the only player ever to win golf's "Triple Crown." This would be Hogan's only trip to play overseas.

Even with his outstanding tournament record, he was still required to qualify to play in the tournament. His early arrival in Scotland caused quite a stir. He came to Scotland determined to win this British Open. With him came his mystique.

"He was a total mystery," said TV commentator Peter Alliss. "He was from another planet. We were all in awe of him. He had an aura. He was like royalty. People would approach him deferentially."

Bordering the golf course was a railway line and beyond that sat the little town of Carnoustie. A crowd of curious onlookers had surrounded the first tee hoping for a glimpse of the golfing legend's first tee shot. As Hogan stepped onto the tee, a passing commuter train slowed, and then made an unscheduled stop, allowing the passenger's a chance to witness this momentous event. There were faces looking from every window.

Carnoustie Golf Course

Sir Michael Bonallack, past British Amateur Champion and Captain of the R&A, in describing Carnoustie once stated;

"When the wind is blowing, it is the toughest golf course in Britain. And when it's not blowing, it's probably still the toughest."

Once you play away from the first tee and clubhouse, the anticipation of playing the famous 585-yard, par five, sixth hole begins to intensify. Defining the left side of the hole is an electric out-of -bounds fence, with signs that warn trespassing out-of-bounds ball searchers that they are now on an active military shooting range. The echoing snap-snap of machine-gun fire, and maybe some intermittent mortar fire off in the distance was an audible con-firmation of that warning.

There are two aptly named "bomb-crater-bunkers" that split the playing area of this hole into left and right fairways. The safer play was towards the much wider right side, but in doing so you eliminate any sensible attempt to get to the green with two shots. To have any chance at hitting the green with two shots, you must drive into the narrow left side fairway.

Hogan chose this risky left side gap between the out-of-bounds fence and the two bunkers every round. His driving accuracy was rewarded by his reaching the green in two shots, producing four birdies. His domination of this hole won the tournament for him. The narrow driving area he had so successively used was quickly nicknamed "Hogan's Alley." And when the Scot's concurred that a man of such courage must surly have ice, and not blood, coursing through his veins, he was affectionately nicknamed "The Wee Ice Man."

50th Anniversary

During a 2003 ceremony celebrating the 50th anniversary of Ben Hogan's Open victory at Carnoustie, the sixth hole was officially dedicated and named "Hogan's Alley." Included that day was a ceremonial long drive contest put on by the participating professionals to honor both Ben Hogan's British Open Victory and his winning of the Triple Crown. The professional participants would use vintage 1953 wood headed drivers and 1.62' diameter golf balls, the same type driver and ball Hogan would have used in 1953.

The long drive results were-

Arjun Atwal 251 yards—driving average today 286.

Paul Lawrie 245 yards—driving average today 290.

Adam Scott 231 yards—driving average today 303

Vijay Singh 219 yards—driving average today 295

The commemorative plague erected at the sixth hole quotes Hogan as saying, "I don't like the glamor. I just like the game."

If only we in golf could again be like that.

BEN HOGAN IS WAITING

Yesterday Today and Tomorrow

Let us set aside the confusion of defining what constitutes the "Grand Slam" in men's pro tournament golf. And let us also set aside the conversation concerning the TPC Championship becoming a major event in golf. Instead, let us take a moment to follow an interesting scoring trend that has been happening in golf through the years. It was Ben Hogan who first suggested that it was physically and mentally possible, and reasonable, to expect a man one day would score eighteen straight birdies.

Points of Interest-2012

+ A score of 60 has been posted in official PGA Tour tournament play twenty-five times.

+ The record for the lowest eighteen-hole score in an official PGA Tour event, 59, has been posted five times, and there has been a scattering of lower scores worldwide.

+ Representing the LPGA, Annika Sorenstam has also scored a 59.

+ Since 2005, the "lowest" score of 55 has been posted twice on regulation-length courses.

Players of Interest

Enter Al Broach—1951

The first round of 60 ever shot on the PGA Tour occurred in the 1951 Texas Open.

Enter Mike Souchak—1955

Mike Souchak, a professional golfer, shot a first-round 60 to win at the 1955 Texas Open at Brackenridge Park South, a public course in San Antonio. His first-round 60 included an era record-breaking 27 on the back nine that held until 2006.

Enter Homero Blancas—1962

Homero Blancas carded a 55 in the 1962 Premier Invitational in Longview, Texas, as an amateur. His score has been brushed aside as a record because the course he played was but a 5,000-yard, nine-hole, par-70 layout, with two different tee boxes per hole. Blancas, an exceptional player, later turned pro and successfully competed on both the PGA and Champions Tours.

Enter Steve Gilley—2005

In 2005, pro golfer and journeyman Steve Gilley made three eagles and ten birdies to shoot 55 at Lynwood Golf and Country Club in Martinsville, Virginia, the lowest verified round of golf ever recorded on a regulation course. He was playing a practice round for the local US Open qualifying.

Enter Rhein Gibson—2012

Australian pro golfer Rhein Gibson recently posted a score of 55 for eighteen holes on River Oaks Golf Course in Edmond, Oklahoma, a 6,800-yard, par-71 regulation golf course. That was 16 under par. Although Gibson was not the first person to shoot 55, he is in select company.

A Matter of Time

Pro Mike Souchak always felt it was just a matter of time until his low score of 60, and his nine-hole record score of 27, would be bettered. Souchak's record-setting score in the 1955 tournament did not attract much attention then, and even today you don't hear his name or his round discussed. As for those four days of tournament golf in San Antonio, they never left Souchak's mind. "I'll remember them to the day I go to the grave," he has said.

The Sands of Time

A noticeable drop in scores has occurred recently. In 2006, Corey Pavin scored 26 for nine holes. In 2005 and 2012, Steve Gilley and Rhein Gibson, respectively, shot their 55s. In the world of golf, that is a lot to take place in a seven-year period. Possibly a harbinger?

What is now proved, was once only imagined. —William Blake

It has taken over fifty years to reduce the game's low score from 60 to 55, so the possibility of Hogan's thoughts coming true is not to be ignored. With the quality of today's players, the excellent condition of the courses, and the improved equipment and golf balls, the opportunity to score low is a reality.

I'm sure Ben Hogan is watching and waiting . . . as we all should be.

TIRED OF TIGER

Tiger Woods, after a missed shot at the Masters, let the club fall from his hands, then turned in anger and kicked it…toward the people in the gallery. This tantrum received plenty of attention at Augusta National.

Even with his antics being edited, he is often seen slamming his club, throwing his club, cursing his club, and pouting over golf shots that are really just a part of the game. And he couldn't care less.

If you think swinging a golf club is hard, throwing or kicking a golf club in anger is much more difficult—and it can be dangerous. Sometimes depicted as a humorous event, club throwing can and has resulted in tragedy.

Juniors

Young people make up a large part of his audience, and they will shadow his every move. They want to throw their clubs like him, spit like him, curse like him. You can witness it at driving ranges, where you can see their "helicopter follow-throughs" and the "uncontrolled club" flying out of their hands after a bad shot. After watching him, they think that anger is cool.

It is not fun to watch.

Weak Apology

During a brief interview with reporters after his round, Woods stood snidely smiling as he offered a weak apology.

"I apologize if I offended anybody by that, but I've hit some bad shots."

(Everyone hits bad shots.)

"It's certainly frustrating at times not to hit the ball where you need to hit it,"

(Everyone gets frustrated.)

"I certainly heard that people didn't like me kicking the club."

(Especially the people you kicked it toward.)

"But I didn't like it, either. I hit it right in the bunker."

(Everyone plays from bunkers.)

"Didn't feel good on my toe, either."

He just can't seem to acknowledge his ongoing rudeness.

A Magician

Just like when he is in trouble on the course, he has these uncanny ways of getting out of all the corners he paints himself into. His caddies, his women, his accidents, all just seem to disappear at the wave of his wallet. His interviews, his answers, are all so rehearsed, banal, and trite. He is so good at hiding.

According to PGA Tour policy, players can be disciplined for "conduct unbecoming a professional." The PGA Tour will not say when or if it disciplines the players, so that policy fits perfectly with Woods because it allows him that wall of silence he so loves to hide behind.

Every network has been burned by his foul language. They cannot seem to impose a monetary penalty large enough to deter his cursing and unacceptable behavior. He just makes too much money—for himself and for others—to concern himself with proper etiquette.

If golf is to remain a gentlemen's game, then we need a "free drop" from this guy. He is not only disrespectful to the game, but also to those he plays with, and to the great players in the past whose generosity built the game and to whom he owes his career.

It was three-time Masters champion Nick Faldo who summarized Tiger's failings the best.

"I think we can officially say Tiger has lost his game . . . and his mind."

WILLIE "TRAP DOOR" JOHNSON

Religious requests for God's intervention during the flight of one's golf ball are very common, and just how different the game might be if these requests were answered. Without positive proof of this intervention, there came a need for caddies.

Men of wealth in eighteenth-century Scotland often employed one or more personal butlers to assist them with their daily duties at home and in the organizing of their travels. On the day that they played their golf, one of those butlers would valet the golf clubs to the course. Once there, he would hand the golf clubs over to a man who knew the secrets of the game: the caddie.

The Role of a Caddie

Betting among the caddies on the outcome of the matches they worked was not uncommon. This monetary competition kept them on their toes, especially when the players hit balls into the high grass or unkempt areas of the course. They would then have to both look for the ball and keep an eye on each other's antics at the same time. These caddies could be very creative in their efforts to either help or hinder finding these lost balls. The role they played would often be the determining factor in the outcome of the match.

The Sandbaggers

Sandbagger is a name describing a thief who would use a sock or a small bag filled with sand to threaten the person whom they were robbing. These sandbags provided the thieves with an effective weapon that could be easily disposed of just by spilling the sand out, leaving no smoking gun for evidence.

Sandbaggers in golf are known for being unusually lucky players who seem blessed with constant good fortune. They are rightfully considered to be the lowest form of player, regardless of their true ability. A good caddie could assume the role of a sandbagger by doing any number of things.

- He could intentionally avoid finding a golf ball.

- He could foil the opponent's good lie by stepping on his ball and pushing it partially into the ground.

- He could step down hard on the ball and totally bury it in soft ground where it would not be found.

Willie "Trap Door" Johnson

It was not uncommon for caddies to be given nicknames. One fabled caddie, Willie Johnson, was nicknamed "Trap Door." The story goes that old Willie had been born with one leg shorter than the other, and because of this handicap he had always worn a special boot. He had his boot specially designed with an enlarged sole that was hollowed out, and with a flap that would open and close like a trap door as he walked.

During any search for balls, Willie would quickly find the ball and step on it, working it into the hollow sole of his boot. Immediately, the ball was "lost." Even for the wealthiest men, a lost golf ball was not a pleasant event, as their cost was nearly equal to a commoner's weekly wage.

Caddie Fee

At the end of their round, you could hear many of the caddies politely reminding their employers of their efforts, saying, "Generosity often leads to loyalty, sir."

You never heard Willie "Trap Door" Johnson remind anyone for extra money. The "lost" golf balls that he now had in his boot would soon be for sale, and when they were sold, they would make a tidy addition to his caddie fee. It was rumored that he could have as many as five extra balls in his boot at a time.

Though many caddies swore that they knew of his scheme, "Trap Door" was never found out.

IMAGINE A FAIR GOLF COURSE

A fair golf course.

Would it be flat like a tennis court or a baseball field?

Would each hole play the same for players of all abilities, like tennis and baseball?

Comparing golf courses and ski slopes would be wiser. They are both built on varying land forms. Ski slopes are rated by their degree of difficulty, while golf courses are rated more for their distance. Golf courses use red tee markers for the shortest course yardage, white tee markers for the medium-length course, and blue tee markers for the longest course. They also use names like "women's," "men's," and "professional" tees. Some modern courses even have "senior" and "junior" tees.

A novice male skier will search out and stay on the easiest slopes when learning to ski. A novice male golfer, unfortunately, would never play from the shortest course, or from the women's or senior tees. If he were to learn to play from the easier tees, like the novice skier, he might enjoy learning to play the game and he might learn to play his golf at a faster pace.

Most recreational golfers do not hit their ball far enough, nor do they manage their games well enough, to play many of today's modern courses. For them, playing the real game of golf would be frustrating and not much fun, so they disguise their bewilderment by estimating their scores and altering the game's penalties. They rarely finish putting. They allow themselves mulligans or do-overs whenever they want. They don't realize that by playing golf in this manner, they are inadvertently endorsing a need for long, difficult golf courses. Long courses with fast greens and tightly cut fairways with high rough are not very enjoyable for most average golfers.

The majority of today's golfers are not long-ball hitters, they are not good putters, and they have trouble hitting shots off tightly cut fairways and out of the high rough. The golfers do have money, and they would like to play golf. Especially if they could enjoy themselves. It looks as though these very necessary recreational golfers have either been forgotten or are being ignored.

After paying his dues, minimums, and other various assessments, today's golfer usually spends five or more hours to play a round of golf. Then he watches as an expensive new tournament tee is constructed to lengthen the most difficult hole on the course. It is explained to him that, "There will be some long-ball hitters playing in this year's championship and we need to challenge their game."

As he watches the digging begin, he wonders instead why they wouldn't replace the forward tee of that hole.

"If they would move it just to the side of the pond, then my wife and kids could hit their balls into the fairway and not the water," he thinks to himself.

That change would please him more.

"Then they might want to join me for a round of golf, followed by dinner at our club. If only they could enjoy themselves. Do the greens really need to be quite that fast?" he wonders.

Just idle thoughts as the backhoe starts digging.

These older classic golf courses should be treated like wonderful works of art. They should be preserved for future generations with their club history and scoring records intact. However, the ruling bodies of golf do not seem interested in or inclined to do this.

There are some that may argue that this did not happen when the feathery golf ball was replaced by the balata golf ball and golf clubs went from having wood to steel shafts, so why should it now? The answer is that golf deserves it, and humankind should feel an obligation to preserve its history.

The money being spent to redesign, lengthen, and modernize these classic courses should be used instead to build modern courses at other locations for use by this minority of golfers. There could be a new game that would accommodate these super-golfers without disturbing the wonderful history of a beautiful game.

If the statistics are correct and golf participation is in a decline, then it seems that it is time for us to change our ways. The majority of golfers have spoken. They don't have the time or the interest to play long, difficult golf courses.

But imagine a fair golf course.

THE GREENBRIER RESORT

After twenty-some years of organizing golf trips to play on the old courses in Scotland and Ireland, I thought it would be fun to visit some of America's "gems." So on I ventured to Bandon Dunes Golf Resort in Oregon, Whistling Straits in Wisconsin, and Sutton Bay in South Dakota. These were new facilities in the world of golf and they were all great, great, great! To make a fair comparison, I thought I should also try the "newest old course" in our country. That took me to the Greenbrier Resort in West Virginia.

I went there to experience the White Hotel surrounded with golf courses, lovely blue mountains, and intriguing stories. Where people came from all over to "take the waters" with hopes of restoring their health. The resort was then known as White Sulphur Springs and was one of the classic railroad resorts of North America.

As I entered the main driveway, the grand white building welcomed me, and the colorful gardens quietly flirted with my senses, begging for my equal attention. Greenbriar is unique, with its own train station . . . horse drawn carriages, the doormen with top hats and their white gloves. This is the place!

The Greenbrier!

I remember hearing stories of a tall, lean, Sam Snead, playing fine golf shots through those West Virginia hills, the lore of his best golf being played sometimes in his bare feet. Through practice and patience, Sam built a long, beautiful golf swing that eventually led him away from the moonshine and into the bright sunshine of professional golf. His remarkable career is enshrined at the Golf Club, where the Sam Snead Restaurant proudly displays memorabilia from his personal collection.

Surrounded by the Allegheny Mountains, the Greenbrier offers not only championship golf, but fine dining, designer boutiques, an indoor heated pool, and a world-class spa. The colorful interior decor, designed by Dorothy Draper, is fun and exciting, and just walking through the hotel is time well spent.

There are many outdoor activities available, including horseback riding, fly fishing, falconry, white-water rafting, and tennis. The Gun Club, located on top Kate's Mountain, offers trap and skeet fields and a ten-station sporting clays course. Try them all. It's a great experience.

Carved deep into the mountainside beneath the hotel is a fallout shelter that was once a top-secret US government relocation facility. The Greenbrier Bunker is now open to anyone interested in reliving a legendary piece of the Greenbrier's history. A bunker tour is an entertaining aspect of the Greenbrier that no other resort can offer you.

Recently built beneath the hotel is the fun and first-class Casino Club. The gaming room is entertaining, convenient, yet exclusive. Luck be a lady tonight!

Dining can be a casual evening at the Prime 44 steakhouse, named for basketball great Jerry West, or you can enjoy the elegance of the main dining room. There you will be dazzled with custom-made chandeliers, stately columns, and magnificent arched windows bringing the ambiance of a dignified Southern mansion to life. This is the evening where you will want to dress to impress—the gentlemen dapper in their coats and ties, the women lovely in their evening dresses. This is a popular part of the Greenbrier experience. Live piano and violin music, candlelight, great food, and fine wine are all available for those who wish to enjoy an evening of formal dining and appreciate that the experience is still being offered.

COBBS CREEK-THE CROWN JEWEL

A Historic Stage

The city of Philadelphia exists as a historic stage. It offers a great opportunity for our young people to visit the Liberty Bell, the Constitution Center, art museums and cultural centers. One and all, they are grandiose, and for this we are blessed.

The Philadelphia area is also well known for its food, such as Philadelphia cream cheese, cheese steaks, and pretzels. We are near oceans, bays, rivers, and creeks, and not too far from both the Big Apple and the US Capitol. Every year Philly is picked up, dusted off, and re-pumped with self-confidence. To live in Philadelphia and not live well is a misfortune.

Yet there sit our city golf courses, quietly yearning for equal attention.

Cobbs Creek Golf Course

It is possible that one of the city courses, Cobbs Creek, has hosted more golf than any other course in the Philadelphia area. It has been kindly and correctly nicknamed "the crown jewel of the city courses." Cobbs has a place in this area's past golf history, and, with a little luck, it will also be a part of its future. The course has hosted PGA Tour events, countless amateur golf events, and has been touted in numerous travel publications as a "must play" golf course for golfers visiting Philly, its "casual conditions" courteously being overlooked. With some creativity and care, this classic jewel of a layout could again become a valuable asset for the city.

Harding Park Golf Course

Through the efforts of local businesses, political leaders, and the San Francisco Park and Recreation, Harding Park Golf Course in San Francisco underwent a monumental restoration and has again become a worthy asset for that city. The "new" course was refurbished as a "fair" golf course for the average player, with generous fairways and medium-length holes. Yet it still can offer a championship-caliber layout when it is called upon. The course was just dusted off and dressed up, and may be re-pumped with some self-confidence.

Interesting Similarities

– Harding Park opened in 1925. Designed by architect Willie Watson of Olympic Golf Club fame, it also offers a shorter Fleming course.

– Cobbs Creek opened in 1916. Designed by Hugh Wilson of Merion Golf Course fame, it also offers a shorter Karakung course.

– Harding Park has hosted major amateur tournaments, the USGA National Public Links Championship, and the San Francisco City Championship.

– Cobb's Creek has hosted major amateur tournaments, the 1928 USGA Amateur Public Links tournament, and a PGA Tour event, the 1955 Philadelphia Inquirer Open.

Unfortunately, another similarity they share is that during periods of city budgetary cuts, both courses fell into disrepair.

Diamond in the Rough

Like the other historical and cultural attractions of the Philadelphia area, Cobbs Creek should also be featured. With some creativity and care, this classic jewel of a layout, could shine like a diamond in the rough.

All we have to do is to pick it up, dust it off, and dress it up . . . and re-pump it full of self-confidence.

PINEHURST
AMERICA'S FIRST GOLF RESORT

The 2014 US Men's Open and Women's Open will be played at Pinehurst Resort and Country Club in Pinehurst, North Carolina. This is the first time the two national championships will be contested on the same course and played on back-to-back weeks. The selected course to host these events is Pinehurst's famous No. 2 Course.

The course setup from week one to week two will require less work than usual, as the concession stands, corporate hospitality suites, and media tents will already be in place. The fairways will already be lined with ropes to guide the galleries, and the grandstands will be in place, so changing the pin locations and the tee markers will be the only necessary course alterations.

Land of the Pines

In 1895, "Pinehurst," or "the wooded hillock covered with beautiful pine trees," was the name owner James Tufts thought best suited his new resort. Over deforestation had left much of the sand hills of North Carolina barren, and it was a bit of a gamble by Tufts to buy the remnants of what was at one time a flourishing pine forest. He envisioned a New England style village, with walkways and year-round greenery; a peaceful place where middle-class Americans could come to recuperate from the feared respiratory illnesses of the time. He thought his new health spa and resort, along with the area's "pine ozone," could offer relief for those ailing people. In 1901, the resort's breathtaking hotel, the Carolina, later tagged the "White House of Golf," opened its doors, and Pinehurst was on its way to becoming "America's First Golf Resort."

Donald Ross

A defining moment in Pinehurst's history also came at the turn of the century with Tuft's hiring of Scotsman Donald Ross. Tufts gave Ross the authority to supervise, oversee, and develop all the golf courses at his resort. Ross maintained this association for the remainder of his life, even though he went on to design hundreds of other courses throughout the nation. Of all of his many course designs, he spoke most often of his beloved No. 2 Course at Pinehurst. It was his masterpiece, a source of much pride, and, for him, a constant "work in progress."

Two other interesting Pinehurst legacies provided by Ross are;

+ "Maniac Hill," the first designed practice ground or driving range ever.

+ The Pine Crest Inn on Dogwood Street in the Village. Ross owned and operated the inn until his death, and it remains a charming establishment in Pinehurst.

America's First Golf Resort

For more than a century, Pinehurst has been a sought-after destination for people from around the world who would come to play this area's forty-plus outstanding golf courses. Once there, they would find not only golf, but also a tidy village, pristinely adorned with beautiful white dogwood flowers, pine cones nearly a foot long, and brilliant red cardinal birds playfully flitting from tree to tree. A peaceful place just as Tufts had envisioned.

It is only fitting that "America's First Golf Resort" should host this unusual combination of our two national championships. Donald Ross would be proud to know that his No. 2 Course is still considered a masterpiece—and that it continues to be a "work in progress."

THE HIGHLAND LINKS
GOLF COURSE

If you travel nearly to the tip of Cape Cod, Massachusetts, you will be in an area that is called the Outer Cape. Here you will find the little town of Truro, which is considered to be one of the more exclusive towns on the Cape. Noticeably, there are many modern looking houses in this area, and this is not following the customary Cape-cottage designs for which coastal New England is famous. The traditional cottages are covered with wooden clapboard that in time becomes an earthy gray color. A color that blends comfortably into the landscape of rolling hills and sandy dunes that are so characteristic of the Cape.

Highland Lighthouse
Truro is also home for Highland Light Station, Cape Cod's oldest lighthouse. Through the years as the lighthouse worked its maritime magic, the wind and sea gnawed away at the surrounding cliffs, eroding the sand and soil and threatening to dump the lighthouse into the Atlantic Ocean. As the edge of these shore cliffs inched closer to the Light Station there came a need to rescue it from sure ruin. In 1996, it was moved away from the cliffs to a much safer location and that happened to be on the Highland Links Golf Course.

Highland Links Golf Course
The Highland Links Course is one of America's golf treasures. It is the oldest golf course on Cape Cod, and though there are but nine holes, two distinct sets of tees can be played totaling just over 5000 yards. But knowing the yardage

of these holes is not as important as knowing what shots you will need to play. Depending on the strength of the near-constant winds, you will face some shots that you may never have played before, and there will be some shots that you may never need to play again. So enjoy the creative opportunity.

Highland Links is not a long golf course, but it will test your ability to navigate a ball down non irrigated fairways, and through moody sea breezes that will taunt you and often bully your shots. Each hole is framed with deep rough, plentiful Scotch broom, and windswept bluffs that decorate the gently rolling fairways. You will find that some of golf's fashionable words, such as plush and manicured, will not be needed when you tell others of your experience at Highland Links.

This is golf played on land left behind by harsh weather and a receding sea. Golf that is accompanied by the intermittent calls of squawking sea gulls and the sounds of crashing waves.

The Others Links Courses
The Highland Links Golf Course is one of only five true links courses in North America. These five links courses are all found in remote areas that can be hard to get to. They are all worth the effort.

Bandon Dunes Golf Resort, located on the Pacific Coast of south west Oregon, is host to three of these links courses. The easiest and most enjoyable way to get to Bandon is to play your way south from Portland. This is a state that offers much great golf. Some fine courses can be found on the coast, some will be found inland.

The most recent addition to this select group of links courses is newly opened Cabot Links on the western coast of Nova Scotia, near the town of Inverness. Cabot Links plays through the sprawling hills near the West coast of Cape Breton Island along the Gulf of St. Lawrence. This a links course where you will enjoy an ocean view on every hole.

So treat yourself to some great golf, and play these five links courses.

ISLAY AND UIST

Not all who wander are lost.
—JRR Tolkien

I opted for a window seat so I could take in the bucolic splendor of the bonnie braes we would pass while touring through Scotland. When the bus paused at the first roundabout, right below my window was a large black cow. She was stretching her neck through a wire fence grazing on the grass closest to the roadway. This amusing scene gave a new meaning to the old adage, "The grass always looks greener . . ." Then I realized that I was no different from that big black cow, searching out old links golf courses on the most remote islands of Scotland.

The Hebrides

In 1891, two golfing masterpieces were created. Both were on remote islands in the Hebrides. The one, named Machrie, was on the island of Islay. The other, named Askernish, was on the island of South Uist. These western islands display stunning scenery, have abundant wildlife and offer the best landscapes, maybe in the world, for great golf courses. Though they may be difficult to get to, they should not be missed.

Islay

Pronounced eye-la, she is known as the Queen of the Hebrides. Traveling to Islay can be difficult no matter how you choose to get there. Once there, you will find that both the island and the Machrie Golf Course are extraordinary.

I was warmly greeted by Liam, the bellman at the Machrie Hotel. He was much younger than I would have expected, though he answered my inquiries with a wisdom usually associated with an older, more experienced person.

Liam told me that the local weather could become quite unsettled making the golf at Machrie unpredictable. He nodded towards the distant mountains saying, "That is our sister island, Jura. If you can see Jura," he forewarned, "that means it's going to rain." Then Liam winked at me and added, "And if you can't see Jura, that means its already bloody raining."

He went on to politely apprise me that the golf would be far from American-style golf. "The grass here is kept short by rabbits and sheep." Then he went on to explain that, "The golf at Machrie, like the malt whisky we produce on Islay, is meant to be savored." Then with a little grin he said, "Just take your swings, and your swigs, and let the wind guide you. You'll find Machrie to be wonderful."

South Uist

In 1891, on the beautiful island of South Uist in the Outer Hebrides of Scotland, the world's greatest golf course designer of that time, Old Tom Morris, produced a golfing masterpiece. Along that coastline, on a stretch of rich fertile land, he built his Askernish Golf Club. Looking out over the dunes, all brimming with flowers and wildlife, Old Tom felt that this coastal area offered the perfect environment for a great golf course.

When the island went through rough economic times, the Askernish course was abandoned. Finally surrendering itself to nature, the course slowly became blanketed with wind blown sands and sea grasses. For years it was forgotten.

Considered by some to be golf's "holy grail," it has recently been rescued, renovated and reopened. In 2008, Old Tom Morris's layout was back in play and fully restored. The course today is being played, discussed, and correctly reviewed as one of the finest links golf courses in all of Scotland.

The Askernish Golf Club is now hosting the Askernish Open, a major event both for South Uist and the Scottish Golfing calendar. This three day tournament draws a field of players from not only the United Kingdom, but also North America and the rest of Europe.

Liam's Wisdom

So when you decide to go wandering, maybe searching out old links golf courses on the most remote islands of Scotland, keep in mind the advice young Liam offered me.

"Just take your swings, and your swigs, and let the wind guide you." You'll find life to be wonderful.

That has surely worked well for me.

THE MASTERS' SECRETS—2012

Bobby Jones first named it "the Augusta National Invitation Tournament." Clifford Roberts wanted to call it "the Masters." Jones thought that sounded presumptuous, but he demurred, and "Masters" it is.

Bobby Jones has been the club's only president—and he remains so in perpetuity. After Jones's death, Roberts assumed total responsibility over the club and the tournament for the remainder of his life.

Clifford Roberts had an unbending manner, and he refused to grant special favors for anyone. Sam Snead, once yarning about local legends, recalled: "Roberts was a real stickler. One time Arnold Palmer went down there with his dad to play golf. Roberts told Palmer that his dad couldn't play unless he was with a member." (Palmer eventually was invited to become a member.)

It was Roberts who was credited for the razor-sharp yearly updating of the Masters. The elaborate leader board that shows how a player stands to par, the tee-to-green gallery ropes, the grandstands, and complimentary pairing sheets were all Masters firsts.

Byron Nelson reminisced: "The ropes were all white. I was out on the course with Cliff, and he looked around at the white ropes and said, 'That doesn't go in this place at all. The ropes should be green.' This was just before the tournament was to start, but in a couple of days the ropes were changed to green."

Not known for his humor, Roberts did have his fun. He once created a film that showed him making a hole-in-one on the par-3 sixteenth hole. As the ball rolled into the cup, the film shows Roberts calmly walking on the water over to the green. On his way, he waved back for his caddie to follow him, and as the caddie tried, he fell head first into the pond. Roberts had built a bridge just below the surface of the water that he would walk on and his caddie would miss.

Things They Won't Talk About

You must be invited to join the club and, until 2012, only men had been invited. Yet, it made you wonder why as the club's ornate gardening did gravitate toward the eye of the gentler sex. The towering pines, fronted with multitudes of azaleas, wisteria, and dogwoods, bloom on command each spring into brilliant pink, fuchsia, and white. Even the main drive into the club is called Magnolia Lane, plantings not necessarily associated with male tastes.

Then there is the speed of the greens; this, their best kept secret.

Here is an amusing story, as told to me about my friend's first round at Augusta.

"I was warned by my host to act respectably, as all eyes would be on us while we ate our lunch in the grill room. After eating, he escorted me to the locker room, where I could change my shoes. By then, I felt like a condemned man being led to the gallows—my nerves were frayed."

(The plot thickens.)

"With nervous fingers, I firmly tied each shoelace, not wanting them to ever come undone again, and once completed I quickly stood up and let out a big sigh—right into the face of the locker-room attendant!"

(The butler did it.)

"Neither of us spoke a word, until at last I broke the ice by asking him, 'Are the greens really as fast as they say they are?'

"Still standing there nose to nose, the attendant politely replied, 'Sir, you have already hit it too hard.'"

You see, there are some things they just won't talk about at Augusta.

TPC–THAT LITTLE ISLAND GREEN

In the beginning, around the turn of the century, someone created a short golf hole on Baltusrol Golf Course in New Jersey. The putting green of that hole was encircled by a trench of water, making it the first "moat hole" in golf. No one really knows whose idea it was, or who designed the hole, but the blame fell on the club's pro.

A few years later, the moat hole was deemed unnecessary, and that sparked a redesign of the entire golf course by architect A. W. Tillinghast, and the moat hole was eliminated. Ironically, A. W. Tillinghast had, just the year before, designed a moat hole of his own at the Galen Hall Golf Course near Reading, Pennsylvania. That green, still being played today, is believed to be the oldest water-surrounded green in existence.

Then the short ninth hole at the Ponte Vedra Club in Florida, also surrounded with water, became the first "island green," and from that blueprint, the infamous "island green" at the TPC Sawgrass facility was created.

Growing Pains

The TPC "island green" has had a hard time growing up. Early on, many players expressed their dislike for the entire TPC golf course by taking their vengeance out on the little 130-yard hole. Their opinions were often less than polite.

"They messed up a perfectly good swamp," one player barked.

Words like "unfair," "carnival golf," and "screwy" were just a few of the grouses snarled by the best players in the game.

There was even a statement issued by a local sea gull. After a player had hit a tidy approach shot that uncharacteristically stayed on the green, a sea gull swooped down next to the ball. After numerous failed attempts to pick up the player's ball, the gull gave it his best peck and finally managed a clumsy takeoff with the ball in his beak. Heroically, he carried the ball away from the green, only to suddenly drop it into the water, much to the amusement of all that were watching. His statement could not have been clearer.

No Charity Needed Here

The seventeenth hole at the TPC has been paying its own way; there's no need to pass the plate. This little guy has become a profit center for both the tournament and the resort. And like it or leave it, this hole won't be going anywhere soon.

It is estimated that each year, 120,000 balls don't make it to the green from the tee. That is an average of three balls per player, for both professionals and tourists alike.

With the tourists, it has become a rite of passage. For them, hitting the green is like kissing the Blarney Stone. Anxiously, without regard for the cost of their golf balls, they elect to keep hitting until their ball stays on the green.

During the Players Championship, the amphitheater-style seating supplies an unobstructed view of each shot. This has attracted corporate people that savor the coliseum atmosphere where they can view, and wager on, each player's efforts, nearest to the hole or nearest the water. A rowdy atmosphere—and so not like golf.

That Little Island Green

Truly, it's not the hole that will beat you. It's the walk from the sixteenth green to the seventeenth tee. It's a hard, serious walk. And it affords you too much time to think about the shot that you have been thinking about all day.

Be it a moat or be it an "island green," we all love a chance to beat the odds. We just can't wait to have at it. Again. And again. And again.

That little "island green." The one we all love to hate.

MERION'S WICKER BASKETS—2012

The 2013 US Open Championship will be held at the historic Merion Golf Club in Ardmore, Pennsylvania. This will be the fifth Open contested at Merion and the first since 1981. Through the years, Merion's East and West Courses have provided us with championship golf events and champion golfers. The club's dining patio, right next to the first tee; the Scottish-style bunkers known as the "white faces of Merion"; those mysterious wicker baskets that decorate each hole—all contribute to the club's mystique.

Wicker Baskets

Those wicker baskets, unique to Merion's East Course, sit conspicuously on top of what are usually called flag poles. The baskets have been a part of Merion's East Course's lore since 1912. As the story goes, the course's architect, Hugh Wilson, while studying the design of various golf courses throughout England, noticed that the local shepherds held staffs that had wicker baskets at one end in which they carried their lunch. His use of the baskets on his East Course was to locate the hole while concealing the direction and strength of any wind, thereby adding a special degree of difficulty to the course.

Golf before the Feathery

One of the legends about the origin of golf, was that it may have first been played by shepherds somewhere in the Highlands of Scotland. While they grazed their flocks in the Highlands, the shepherds carried herding staffs called shillelaghs. These shillelaghs were fashioned from tree limbs and typically had a large knob on the top end. Used also as walking aids, these sticks helped the shepherds traverse the rocky, rain-soaked, and often muddy hillsides. They also used them to move their flocks from pasture to meadow, and as weapons when protecting their herd from common predators such as wolves.

There were certain mountain walking paths in the Highlands that were more important than others. These were the paths that would lead to water, be it either a simple running stream or a deep well somewhere in the wilderness. These common pathways would often become littered intermittently with droppings of sheep excrement. To clear the way, the young herders would casually flick the chunks of dung out of their way using the knob end of their shillelaghs. When they came upon older, dried-out chunks of manure, they would take more forceful swings with their shillelaghs and then marvel at the dung as it flew high and far, down into the valleys. They called their new diversion *"shootin' the shite."* Ultimately, *"shootin' the shite"* evolved into the game we today call golf.

Golf after the Feathery

In due course, the shepherds designed special wooden clubs that replaced the shillelaghs. They also handcrafted a new ball from goose feathers they found scattered near the lochs. These feathers were tightly packed into a wet cowhide sphere, and when it dried, the leather shrank and the feathers expanded, creating a hardened ball. What a welcome change from those old original sheep droppings!

The shepherds, with these new implements, no longer needed the knob-headed shillelaghs for that purpose, so they attached wicker baskets on them and used them to carry and protect their lunch from marauding ferrets and other hungry creatures. The shepherds could now leave their shillelaghs unattended when searching for their new feathery balls that they so enjoyed hitting through the flower-dappled meadows.

The Rest of the Story

As you can see, this wonderful game may have really started not on the sea side links-lands, but instead somewhere deep in the Highlands of Scotland. And those wicker baskets you see today at Merion Golf Club, they are mere artifacts from those early days, when golf was in its infancy and struggling to evolve.

So now (maybe) you know the rest of the story.

THE TWO MUIRFIELDS

Golf was first played at Muirfield in 1891 on eighteen holes laid out by Old Tom Morris.

Golf was also first played at Muirfield in 1974 on eighteen holes laid out by Jack Nicklaus.

Muirfield—Scotland

Muirfield, the home of the Honorable Company of Edinburgh Golfers, may be the most historic and important club in the entire world. The Muirfield Golf Course was originally laid out by Old Tom Morris in 1891 and renovated by Harry Colt in 1923. It was Colt who introduced the two loops of nine holes each.

Muirfield Golf Club is a links golf course with an unusual layout. True links courses have an "outward" nine running in one direction along the coast, and an "inward" nine which returns alongside, but in the opposite direction. The direction of the coastal winds offers opposite and often opposing wind patterns as you play out and back.

The Muirfield Golf Club layout, however, is arranged differently. On this course, the holes follow a circular routing and consist of two loops of nine holes each. One loop runs clockwise; one counterclockwise. Combine this arrangement with the area's prevailing winds and you will find differing wind conditions for nearly every shot! Of all the Open courses, it is thought that this course is the fairest test of championship golf. It has been said that the great players always play great there. The course is known as fair, with no tricks or blind shots. It offers just pure golf.

Muirfield to host the 2013 Open Championship

Muirfield Golf Club hosted the first seventy-two-hole Open Championship in 1892. The course has since been host to eleven Amateur Championships and, in 2013, for the sixteenth time, it will again be the venue for the British Open Championship. Recently lengthened to combat today's longer-hitting players, the course remains a fair and enjoyable test of golf for the average player.

Nicklaus and Muirfield

While spectating at the 1926 Amateur Championship at Muirfield, Scotland, George Herbert Walker was so impressed with the sportsmanship displayed in the final match that he visualized a continuing contest between the top amateurs in America and Great Britain and Ireland. These matches became known as the Walker Cup.

Jack Nicklaus first played Muirfield during his participation in the 1959 Walker Cup, and seven years later, he won his first British Open title there. So, taken by the golf course, Nicklaus brought the memories of these victories home and proudly named his new course in Ohio "Muirfield Village."

Muirfield Village to host the 2013 Presidents Cup

Along with the annual Memorial Tournament, Muirfield Village will also play host to the 2013 Presidents Cup. This will be the third "Cup" competition to be hosted at this facility, the other competitions being the Ryder Cup in 1987 and the Solheim Cup in 1998.

Having this Presidents Cup at Muirfield Village offers a special opportunity to honor Jack Nicklaus, the captain of the US team on four occasions.

Having these matches at his club also offers him a grand way to conclude his career.

"It will probably be my last involvement in anything significant in the game of golf," he has said.

The Presidents Cup is coming to Muirfield Village in 2013 to honor a man who loved his game and to help him gather his memories, one more time.

GHOSTS OF ST ANDREWS

The Relics of St Andrews

Saint Rule, a medieval Greek monk, was warned by an angel, during a dream, that the buried remains of St Andrew were in danger and he was needed to transport them to the 'ends of the earth' for safe keeping. He reacted to the angels warning by retrieving and removing the box that contained the remaining parts of St Andrew; the three fingers of his right hand, the upper bone of an arm, one kneecap, and one of his teeth. Then, with box in hand, he immediately sailed away, in search of a safe harbor.

His pilgrimage brought him to the treacherous coastal waters off of Scotland, where shipwrecked, he was forced to come a shore bringing with him the relics. There, he constructed a special chapel where he secretly hid these relics of St Andrew. This chapel would later become the Cathedral of St Andrews.

The Plague

During the Plague of 1605, the remains of many of the victims were disposed of in the Cathedral of St Andrews, and in 1868, it was decided to completely seal off the abbey. Soon thereafter, a female apparition was seen by many of the towns residents, silently gliding along the outside wall of the Castle in a flowing white gown and elbow length white leather gloves. The spirit became known as the "White Lady."

The White Lady

During the reformation, there was a beautiful young woman that committed heresy, and was imprisoned. During her incarceration, she was tortured and burned, her face becoming hideously disfigured. The apparition seen roaming the Cathedral grounds was thought to be her restless spirit, and at days end, the towns people avoided going near the "haunted tower" for fear of an encounter with this frighteningly grotesque ghost.

These fears prompted an investigation, and two stonemasons were commissioned to search out any hidden rooms or secret passages in the Cathedral. Through these excavations, a sealed vault containing numerous coffins was discovered. Upon opening one of the coffins, they found that it contained a well preserved mummified body of a young woman wearing a white gown with a cross shaped locket round her neck, and she was wearing white leather gloves! Subsequent investigations were hampered when the body suddenly and mysteriously disappeared! The vault was soon resealed and the stonemasons evacuated the area, never to return.

'Neath a Simple Stone

If you tour the St. Andrews Cathedral Cemetery, you will have the opportunity to pay your respects to Old Tom and Young Tommy Morris, both four time winners of the British Open.

It was 1875, Old Tom and Tommy Morris were participating in an exhibition golf match at North Berwick Golf Course when Tommy received notice that his wife of one year, Margaret, who was heavy with child, had become dangerously ill. He returned to his home post haste, only to find that both Margaret and his newborn infant son had both died an hour earlier.

Young Tom Morris' grief was insurmountable. He stopped eating, began drinking heavily and, within months, the twenty-four year old joined his wife and son in death and they are buried as a family in the Cathedral Burial Grounds.

"People said he died of a broken heart." Old Tom recalled. Then he angrily recanted that saying, "If a broken heart could kill you, I would have died also."

Old Tom Morris outlived his son by thirty years and is "lying 'neath a simple stone," only a few clubs lengths from his Young Tommy's family tomb.

These are the infamous Ghosts of St Andrews Cathedral.

THE SPIRITS OF THE OLYMPIC CLUB

The game of golf, like many other sports, has its fair share of "quirky" rituals and strange superstitions, such as the color of the clothes you wear, the number ball that you play, or even the coins used to mark the ball. Some players use only white tees; others won't use white tees at all. Some even avoid superstitions altogether, citing bad luck!

Restless Spirits

The "spirits" of the Lake Course at the Olympic Club in San Francisco, where the 2012 US Open was played, seemed to challenge these superstitions. They cast their spells on the leading golfers, altering their pathway toward an enchanting victory with heartbreaking defeat.

1955 Open

This was the first time the Lake Course hosted the US Open. In this championship, a relatively unknown municipal course pro, Jack Fleck, birdied two of the last four holes to tie the already (erroneously) announced victor, Ben Hogan. This forced an eighteen-hole Sunday playoff, where he corrected history by formally defeating Hogan for the title.

The Spirits Say

Fleck, while shaving that morning, looked in the mirror and heard a voice say, "Jack, you are going to win the Open." He would later tell people: "It just came out and I heard it. I felt the Lord must have been talking to me." With Fleck's revelation, so began the Lake Course's reputation for producing unlikely winners and losers.

1966 Open

During this US Open Championship, fan favorite Arnold Palmer dominated the field, leading by seven strokes with only nine holes left to play. Billy Casper trailed Palmer by five shots as they approached the fifteenth hole, and then two holes later they were tied; Casper later trounced Palmer by four strokes in the eighteen-hole playoff.

"People close to me and close to him say he was never the same again," says Casper.

The Spirits Say

Palmer, in his attempt to break the Open scoring record, lost sight of the tournament and his possible victory. That evening, eerie whispers and low laughter were heard deep in the dark shadows of the course's cypress trees. Was it the spirits of the Lake Course boasting of another great upset? Palmer never won another major.

1987 Open

The Olympic Club, now with a reputation for being hostile to legends, again played host to the US Open. With birdies on the fourteenth, fifteenth, and sixteenth holes, Scott Simpson overtook sentimental favorite Tom Watson, winning the Open by a shot and without the need for a playoff.

The Spirits Say

The spirits concluded that if Fleck beat Hogan, and Casper beat Palmer, then it would only be fair that Simpson beat Watson. At that moment, Scott Simpson skulled his third shot from a green side bunker and his ball was mystically snagged by the flag, dropping down just feet from the hole, allowing him to make par. It was just the change in his luck that he needed.

1998 Open

Payne Stewart carried a four-stroke lead into Sunday's final round, but that was not enough. Lee Janzen came from behind to become the champion.

The Spirits Say

With the legacy of Hogan, Palmer, and Watson looming before him, Janzen, at the par-4 fifth, pushed his tee shot into the cypress trees right of the fairway, and his ball stayed in a tree. As he was walking back to the tee to play another ball, a gust of wind kicked up and his ball mysteriously tumbled out of the tree. This break was followed by Janzen's unbelievable chip shot that went in for a par on that hole. It was just the change in luck that he needed.

2012 US Open

Webb Simpson sat staring in disbelief at the locker-room television (the modern version of a mirror), watching as he emerged from the fog-filled final round victorious over the two favorites, Jim Furyk and Graeme McDowell. After the presentation of the trophy, in keeping with an Olympic tradition, the spirits gently buried them both in that, "graveyard of champions."

RYDER CUP—2012

The 39th Ryder Cup Matches were held at the Medinah Country Club in Medinah, Illinois, marking the first time the Ryder Cup has been played in Illinois.

Ryder Cup History

In 1922, a match play competition began between the American and British amateur golfers called the Walker Cup. Once the Walker Cup was successfully established, the conversation turned towards starting a similar event limited to professional golfers. In 1927 a biennial competition between professional golfers representing the United States and Great Britain was started, called the Ryder Cup.

Spectating the Ryder Cup

The Ryder Cup may be the last great professional sporting event where winning, and not prize money, is its own reward. The 24 man competition has become one of the most popular modern sporting events, drawing large supportive galleries when played in either Europe or the United States. With just six groups playing, and all at similar times, watching these players compete can be exhilarating. You can start out following your favorite players and easily change to watch the other matches, letting the excitement of the day lead you. With galleries that are never shy when offering appreciation for their favorite team's efforts, the entire competition can be electrifying.

The Ryder Cup Format

The Ryder Cup takes place over three days and includes foursomes, four ball, and singles matches.

A *Foursome* Match: The golfers compete in teams of two, using one ball, and taking alternate shots until the hole is completed. One player will take the tee shot on odd-numbered holes, and the other on even-numbered holes.

A *Four Ball* Match: There are two teams of two players. Each golfer plays his own ball throughout the round. A team's score for a given hole is the lower score of that team's players on that hole.

Slowly Does It Every Time

If you followed the 2012 Ryder Cup, you were privy to an exceptionally spirited European victory. The Championship played out like the fable, *The Tortoise and the Hare*, with the United States Team reaching for the coveted "Cup" on Saturday, while the European Team just kept plodding along to victoriously cross the finish line before them on Sunday.

The US Team was cheered on by large, boisterous crowds, while the European team was quietly kept alive by a sentimentality they shared for their recently departed friend and teammate, Seve Ballesteros. Seve's spirit was everywhere; an image on the players clothing, the subject of their stories, and the cause of their tears and laughter. He was both their non-playing captain, and the honorary "thirteenth man" on their team.

A "Poulter-geist"

Englishman Ian Poulter is no stranger to spirits. He once reported that there was a poltergeist roaming the house he had rented while he was playing in Hilton Head, South Carolina.

"Check this out," he relayed to friends. "We have a ghost in our house this week and I'm not joking. We have had some very strange goings on every night." Then he added, "We have a dead bolted door in the house and every morning that door is unlocked and slightly open. It's happened seven times already."

Coincidentally, it had been Poulter who acknowledged Seve's presence at Medinah. During a dispirited team meeting one evening, Europe's team Captain Jose Marie Olazabal, during an emotional speech, suggested that, "Seve is here." His words brought silence, and afterwards a confirmation from Poulter.

"It was amazing to see the atmosphere change in that team room," said Poulter. "The spirit, I mean, it just changed. All week we'd been beaten quite clearly, and we just felt there was that little glimmer of hope."

Attempting to explain Europe's extraordinary come from behind victory, Poulter said, "It was Seve looking down on us." Unbelievably, Poulter had birdied the last five holes to win his four-ball match.

"Slowly does it every time!" So said the tortoise.

THE FOUR MAJORS

There are golfers from all over the world who contemplate their successful participation in one of the four major golf tournaments. Should someone magically win all four of these major tournaments in the same calendar year, it is called a "Grand Slam."

Grand Slam

The original four majors were the British Open and Amateur and the US Open and Amateur. In 1930, the revered amateur golfer Bob Jones won all of these in one year, completing what was called the "Grand Slam." With these victories, Jones set a precedent that would never again be duplicated.

In 1934, the Masters was founded and became a "major" event. The "Grand Slam" then meant a player would have to win the titles to four new major championships (the Masters, US Open, British Open, and PGA Championship) in a single calendar year, the US and British Amateurs being set aside.

Walter Hagen

During those early years, pro golfers were looked upon with disdain. They were not allowed to enter most clubhouses, and if they were invited in, they would need to use a back entrance.

However, golf's aficionado, Walter Hagen, changed all that. His winning the PGA Championship five times helped to elevate the tournament to the major status that it still retains today. This exceptional play, coupled with his flamboyant behavior, gave the PGA the credence that it still enjoys today. Fellow pro golfer Gene Sarazen gave praise to Walter Hagen, saying, "All the professionals should say a silent thanks to Walter Hagen each time they stretch a check between their fingers. It was Walter who made professional golf what it is."

His heartfelt comment is still echoed today, but it is reiterated when discussing Arnold Palmer's career and what he did to elevate the modern-day professional golfers. He is credited with the exceptional prize money and extended TV coverage of golf events all around the world.

The Majors

The Masters tournament is the only major played on the same golf course every year. It is thought to be the most prestigious of all the majors, hosts the smallest field, and, like the Kentucky Derby, has become a highlight of the sporting year.

The US Open is touted to be the toughest to win of the majors. The USGA is often criticized by the players for difficult course setups that border on being unfair. The USGA's tournament objective is to have even par be the winning score.

The British Open is played at one of nine select links courses in Scotland and England. This is the oldest of the majors, and it uniquely challenges the competitors with links-style golf.

The PGA Championship is the only major exclusive to pros. It is played at different courses throughout the United States and is the year's final major.

The Modern Grand Slam

In 1960, Arnold Palmer won both the Masters and the US Open early in the season. During a casual discussion with a sports writer, the idea of winning "a Grand Slam of his own" was brought up. All he would need to do is win both the upcoming British Open and PGA Championships to finish off the season. Even though they were not won, the golf media loved this idea. This pursuit of the elusive Grand Slam has been discussed and prophesied by golfers ever since.

In 1953 Ben Hogan became the only player to come close; winning three majors (The Masters, and the US and British Opens) in the same calendar year. Unfortunately, he could not compete in that year's PGA Championship.

A "Career Grand Slam" is winning the four major titles over the course of a male player's entire career. There have been five Career Grand Slams: Gene Sarazen, Ben Hogan, Jack Nicklaus, Gary Player, and Tiger Woods.

UNITED GOLF ASSOCIATION

Until 1961, the golf tournaments run by the Professional Golfers Association (PGA) were only available "for members of the Caucasian race." Then the PGA rescinded its "Caucasians-only" clause, allowing black golfers to play on that tour. This change in policy ended the need for the United Golf Association, and it also closed the door on the saddest period in the history of professional golf.

United Golf Association

While African American pro golfers were being denied participation in the PGA's tournaments, Robert Hawkins, a golfer from Massachusetts, was starting the United Golf Association (UGA), an organization that would provide golf tournaments where those black pros could compete. From these UGA tournaments, many golfing legends would emerge, such as Joe Louis, the former boxing great; Charlie Sifford, the PGA's first African-American touring professional; and Lee Elder, the first African American professional golfer to play in the Masters Golf Tournament. There were other talented black playing professionals like Bill Spiller, Eural Clark, Ted Rhodes and Howard Wheeler who supported the UGA by participating regularly in it's tournaments.

The UGA held tournaments at any course that would have them. The courses were usually average layouts and were often shabby, certainly not the plush courses that pro golf tournaments are known for. Yet, these pros endured these conditions, understanding that when the last putt dropped, there would be a player with the low score for the day, and it very well could be them.

Howard "Butch" Wheeler

Howard Wheeler learned to caddy at a young age at both the Brookhaven Country Club and East Lake Golf Club in Atlanta, Georgia. While caddying, he would watch how the best players would go about swinging their clubs and hitting their shots. Then, after the round, he would find a club to swing and he would mimic them. Even though he was naturally left handed, he learned to play the game using right handed clubs, those being the only clubs he could muster up.

There was little opportunity for advancement from the caddy ranks, but Wheeler did become the Caddie Master at the East Lake Club. He worked hard at that position, and practiced his golf even harder. His reputation as an accomplished, long hitting player preceded him as he started to play in tournaments. In 1931 he won the Atlanta Open, and two years later he won the first of his six National "Negro Open" Championships.

Cobbs Creek Golf Course

Wheeler eventually relocated to Philadelphia, and Cobbs Creek Golf Club became his home course. While playing at Cobbs Creek, he would find a steady stream of highly competitive money games which helped him become a more accomplished player.

His most competitive matches were against the two-time Philadelphia Open Champion, Bud Lewis, longtime club pro at the Manufacturer's Golf Course, in Oreland, PA, and a touring professional named Charlie Sifford, who became the first African American to play on the PGA Tour. Sifford would later become the first and only black professional to be inducted into the World Golf Hall of Fame.

In 1947 at Cobbs Creek Golf Course, Howard Wheeler won the fourth of his six National "Negro Open" titles. His winning score was four shots lower than that of Charlie Sifford. Ironically, it seemed only fitting that Wheeler should win, as it was under his tutelage that Sifford had become such an outstanding professional player.

Many of today's professional golfers owe their careers to these great trailblazing champions. It was their patience, perseverance, and moral courage, that opened the doors to the glamor and prize monies that today's players enjoy.

These golfing legends and the hardships they endured should not be forgotten.

HOW TO USE GOLF CLUBS

Every day you can hear golfers lament about their high-tech clubs. They say things like, "They are extra big, extra long, and extra light . . . and they don't work!" Could it be that they are not using them correctly?

When we buy golf equipment, we are sold on all the technological advances that clubs have a large sweet spot, the weight of the shaft, the type of materials that make up the club head and shaft, but they don't explain how to use the clubs. There should be directions included when you buy golf clubs, similar to when you buy a computer, even though no assembly is required. The directions are the first thing you see when you open the box of a new computer.

When you buy golf clubs, regardless of your experience or ability, it is assumed that you know the basics of using the woods, irons, and even rescue clubs and putters. For those golfers who don't understand these basics, let me provide two tips that should be included in the directions of the new high tech clubs.

There are two parts of a golf club that you should be familiar with: the club head and the grip.

THE CLUB HEAD

The part of the club head that you use to hit the ball is the club face. The club face has different lofts that control the height of your shot.

What are "those lines" on the club face?

The area of the club face closest to the shaft is called the heel.

The area of the club face furthest from the shaft is called the toe.

The line on the club face closest to the ground is called the leading edge.

The face has other lines that go from the heel to the toe, but the leading edge (or bottom line) is the most important. On most clubs, the companies have even painted it white so you will be aware of its position. To be used correctly, a golf club must have its face set square.

To set the face square, you must set the white line or leading edge perpendicular to the target line. Another way to think of it is that the white line or leading edge should point straight away from you as you address the ball. If the leading edge (the white line) points left, the club is shut. If it points right, the face is open.

THE GRIP

A hammer handle is oblong. That oblong shape can be held by a right, or left handed man, woman, or child, and that shape will help each of them to grip the hammer so the head can be used as it was intended. It's uncomfortable to hold a hammer handle incorrectly and try to use it. Per the rules of golf, the grip on a golf club cannot have ridges or forms to guide us with the placing of our hands. When a golf club is built, the club makers depend on the golfer to use that correct hand position, and then they design a club head and shaft combination that will be most effective for hitting a ball. If we insist on using a hand position that differs from the one they use, then the design benefits of their research won't work as well.

WHAT ARE THOSE LINES

You will find that most of the companies have "decorated" the grip with flowery looking designs, diamond shapes, blocks, or whatever other shapes and lines they want. These attractive designs are right on the top of the grip where the golfer can see them. These decorations on the grip are "silent" guides that show us the correct hand and finger placement for the club to work best.

These guides show us where our thumbs should be located, how close to the end of the club our hand can be without losing control. That is if we are to benefit from the club maker's research.

Just like we benefit from the fellow that built the hammer handle when we swing a hammer.

Once you get your hands on the club correctly and set the club face square, then you can start working on your swing again. But by then you may find that you won't need as much help with your swing as you thought.

THE ELUSIVE POT OF GOLF

Like the mythological Phoenix, the debate about belly putting with the anchored putting style appears to burn itself into ashes, and then it somehow renews itself and comes to life again.

The ruling bodies of golf will most likely ban the putting style of anchoring any club to the body while playing a stroke. Anchoring refers to any putting method outside the definition of a natural and traditional stroke. In anticipation of this decision, there are increasing utterances of legal action brought on by the players it may affect.

WHEN NO ONE CARED

It should never have come to this, because this method of putting should have been banned immediately–years ago. But no one really seemed to care.

+ When pro Paul Runyan won the 1936 Belmont Open in Boston, using a long putter anchored to his belly, no one cared. "It was an advantage I hadn't expected," revealed Runyan. " This system minimizes the adverse effect of nervous tension."

+ When Richard T. Parmley patented the belly putter in 1965, no one cared.

+ When pro Phil Rodgers used a belly putter in tournament competition back in the 1967, no one cared.

+ When pro Paul Azinger won the in 2000 Sony Open by seven shots using a belly putter, no one cared.

- When the belly putter was credited with 8 wins on the PGA Tour in 2003, the conversation changed, and there was some serious discussions about this curious style of putting. But that talk fizzled again, because no one cared.

THEN SOMEONE CARED

- Then Keegan Bradley won the 2012 PGA Championship using a belly putter. He enthusiastically responded to the possible banning of this style of putting saying, "I'm going to do whatever I have to do to protect myself and the other players on tour." He cared.

- Then Webb Simpson won the 2012 U.S. Open Championship using a belly putter. "To me, to change something that big could cost club manufacturers millions of dollars. You've got to have some pretty good facts." Simpson cared.

- Then Ernie Els won the 2012 British Open Championship, using a belly putter. Ernie Els, who had once been among the traditionalists that argued against the style, now vented his new supportive feelings saying, "They're going to have a couple of legal matters coming their way." Ernie cared.

- Then Fred Couples followed with a belly putter victory in the 2012 Senior Open Championship. "The long putter and the belly putter, I really think they are okay," added Couples, seemingly unruffled by the entire debate, whose later career was salvaged by these long clubs.

OTHERS COMMENT

Irish pro golfer Padraig Harrington summed it up nicely when he aired his thoughts saying, "If somebody invented the belly putters tomorrow, it would not pass. The only reason it got through is the people who used it 20 years ago were coming to the end of their careers."

Phil Mickelson, good friend of Keegan Bradley commented, "It's just that I don't think you can take away what you've allowed players to use, practice, and play with for 30 years. I think it is grossly unfair."

GO FOR THE GOLD

Belly putters and the anchoring of clubs against one's body will soon be old news, just like when metal headed woods replaced persimmon and the game found a need to ban square grooves on the iron clubs. These equipment corrections are simply reminders that this game needs to protect itself and it's history. And when this issue gets resolved, the game will return to normal. The players will again fly off in pursuit of their next tournament and their share of that very elusive pot of gold, and lest we forget, a pot that's filled with golf's golden history.

THE YIPS

This is a term feared by golfers describing quick, jerky movements that are known to interfere with one's putting stroke. These involuntary wrist and body spasms have been described in terms such as the twitches, the jitters, and the jerks. I even heard a caddy in Scotland call them "the whisky" as he compared one player's shaky putting stroke to the shaky hands one gets from an overindulgence in drink. Nearly half of all golfers have felt these little tremors, and many serious golfers have even experienced these yips in other parts of their game. The yips can become so bad for some golfers that they have to quit playing the game altogether.

FEAR OF FAILURE

Although an exact cause is not known, there are people who believe the yips are caused by biochemical changes in the brain that come with age. Because they can affect both the young and old, I believe the yips are caused more often by a fear of failure. They are similar to experiencing stage fright, where an actor suddenly forgets the words he has rehearsed for so long. The brain elects to freeze rather than face the embarrassment of failure.

GOAL CONFUSION

These involuntary flinches may be happening because you are pursuing two separate goals at the same time. Your first goal is to have the putter and ball contact each other perfectly. Your second goal is to help the ball to go in the cup. During the stroke, as the putter nears the ball, your eyes anticipate that contact is imminent and they immediately switch to look for the cup. This quick change of thought creates confusion. It's like trying to rub your stomach and pat your head at the same time. When you do either one of those things by themselves, they are simple tasks. Yet when you try to do them both at the same time they are confusing. The yips are born in this confusion.

THE CURE

To cure the yips, some right-handed golfers will try putting left-handed. Some other players will change the size of their putter grip or re-weight the head of their putter. Some may change to a long putter, or a belly putter, or they may try putting with their eyes closed. The list goes on and on.

The suggestion that I make to people suffering with the yips is for them to maintain a constant grip pressure on the club throughout the stroke. This will help to eliminate these flinches.

Next I suggest that the golfer look at the cup instead of the ball while he putts. This helps to eliminate the anxiety of trying to guide the putter face squarely into the ball. These two simple diversions will help to calm the hands so a smooth putting stroke becomes possible.

Now, if you want to know how to pat your head while rubbing your stomach....

GOLF COLLECTORS

GOLF MEMORABILIA

The earliest known reference to a set of golf clubs being specially crafted for a particular golfer was a set made for King James VI of Scotland; that was around 1600.

Then if we move forward another 87 years we find that there was a book by Thomas Kincaid titled *Thoughts on Golve.* This book contained the first references on how golf clubs were made.

Then a few years later, in 1691, we find that the town of St. Andrews is referred to in print as the "metropolis of golfing."

These early golf clubs, reference books, and documents have been collected, preserved, and put aside for the enjoyment of future generations. Humanity does have the obligation of preserving its history.

Old golf memorabilia is often carelessly set aside or tucked away in the corners and rafters of sheds, garages, and attics. When these sometimes curious-looking artifacts are again discovered, we should first thank the people that cared enough to at least stow the items away. Then we should be thankful that there is a fraternity of people, the *Golf Collectors Society*, that is committed to maintaining and keeping golf's past alive.

THE GOLF COLLECTORS SOCIETY

The Golf Collectors Society (GCS) is an international organization dedicated to preserving the treasures and traditions of the game of golf. Founded in 1970 by Robert Kuntz from Dayton, Ohio and Joseph S.F. Murdoch from Philadelphia, Pa., the organization today has over 1400 members from 15 countries.

Members in this society collect hickory shafted golf clubs, balls, books, tees, ceramics, silver, art, programs, postcards, early golf magazines, and autographs to name just a few. As they are proud to announce, "If it was used in the game of golf, it's likely a GCS member collects it!"

NEW MEMBERS ARE WELCOME

Golf Collectors Society (GCS) members come from a variety of backgrounds. Some collectors are amateur golfers playing the game for fun and some are pros playing the game for a living. There are also golf writers, author's and even some museum curators. But the most important collector is that everyday golfer that lives right down the street. It's that man or women that may be innocently housing a much sought after relic or artifact that would complete a collection.

As a member, you will be kept up-to-date with featured collections, unusual clubs, and artifacts. You will be welcome to attend their Regional Meetings, as well as the Golf Collectors Annual Meeting.

If you would like to be enlightened as to the value of those old golf clubs you found stashed away in your attic, or if you would like to try a round of golf using authentic hickory shafted clubs, the Golf Collectors Society is available to answer your questions.

OAKHURST

Late in the 1800s, in a quiet valley in White Sulphur Springs, West Virginia, there was a group of men that gathered to try their hand at a new game called golf. After a few attempts, Russell Montague and this group of his neighbors developed a strong liking for the game, and by 1884 they had started what became the first golf club in America. As time passed, Montague and most of the original members either passed or moved away leaving the club dormant. For the next 50 years, while the golf shafts went from hickory to steel, and the golf balls from gutta percha to balata, and the golf tees from sand to wood, the little course lay hidden in a pasture of high grasses, valuable to no one but Mother Nature.

Rebirth of a Golf Course

Then in 1960 Lewis Keller bought the property. With some encouragement and prodding from his friend, Sam Snead, he decided to resurrect the old golf course. Keller enlisted noted golf course architect Bob Cupp, and they together researched and restored the nine hole course back to the original 2,235 yards par 34 layout.

Their goal was for the course to be played using hickory clubs and the gutta percha ball, replicating the golfing experience offered to golfers in the 1800s. Keller even kept the grass "mowed" as in the old days, by allowing sheep to graze over the course.

To duplicate the experience of playing golf in the1800s, every golfer was provided with hickory shafted clubs, and replica "gutty" balls, along with instructions on how to use sand tees. Playing the game with these clubs and balls was a fun and often stunning experience for many first timers. These golfers found that the "gutty" would only fly half the distance that todays balls flew. And they also reported that when they hit the "gutty" with a "hickory stick" it felt like they had hit a chunk of dried out peat. Even Sam Snead, after teeing off at the courses grand "reopening" tournament in 1994, smiled back at the applauding gallery and declared, "It sounded like I hit a frog!"

At Auction

If you ever dreamt of owning your own golf course, this was your chance. Even though Oakhurst offers a unique golfing experience, Lewis Keller sadly found that the course was not carrying itself as he had hoped and it went to auction.

With the grandeur of both The Greenbrier and White Sulphur Springs Resorts so near, the undertaking and promoting of a rough and tumble old fashioned course, such as the Oakhurst Links, seemed to most buyers a daunting task.

Then, after Keller's unsuccessful attempts to auction the course off, Jim Justice—owner of The Greenbrier Resort—agreed to buy and operate the "nation's oldest golf course."

"To be perfectly honest," Justice said, " I don't know that it's going to be a great thing for the Greenbrier. But I know it's a great thing to do."

There is little doubt that he was referring to preserving this wonderful game of golf.

PUTTING THROUGH
THE GARDENS

Childhood remembrances like our first day at school, first bike, or even our first kiss, are special events in life that we all love to revisit.

Another special memory producer was playing miniature golf. That was the place where our imaginations would run wild. A place where we would become the giants, towering over the castles and wind mills and waterfalls.

Where we would hit a ball into one hole and watch as it reappeared magically out of one of many tunnels and roll onto another green. Mini golf always amazed us.

It Was 1916

Pinehurst, North Carolina, the home of both America's first golf resort and first golf practice range, was also the home of America's first miniature golf course.

Resident James Barber was looking for a simple form of entertainment that could be played quickly, cheaply, and easily by people of all ages. He imagined a small golf course with holes three yards long instead of three hundred. He figured that the game would require little land, you would only need one club, one ball, and sometimes only one shot.

Barber saw his little course as being a series of natural pathways meandering through the gardens behind his Pinehurst estate. "Garden golf" may have been the proper name, but the story goes that after he played the newly

finished course, Barber remarked, "this'll do" to his gardeners. This spawned
the name of the little course making it, "Thistle Dhu."

It Was 1922

His little course became an immediate hit, and it began to attract even serious golfers. There were so many people playing at "Thistle Dhu," that the
natural grass turf began to wear away.

The game migrated from Pinehurst into the big cities, and an "artificial
green" of a crushed and dyed cottonseed hull carpeting was invented to
reduce maintenance costs. Mini golf was now being played on the rooftops
of city skyscrapers, and in place of Barber's gardens it was now featuring less
expensive obstacles such as little man made bridges, windmills and tunnels.
No longer was miniature golf exclusive to only the elite estate-owners and
expensive resorts. Mini golf is now being marketed to the masses.

To prevent the players from playing additional holes without buying another
game, the last hole was designed to capture the ball. The tease being that if
you hit the ball into that special hole, maybe a clown's mouth, a bell would
ring and you would win a free game.

It Was 1927

Garnet Carter was the first person to patent a game of miniature golf. He
called it "Tom Thumb Golf" and successfully offered franchises to interested
investors. His mini golf game was a big hit with the public and was even
affecting attendance at the very popular movies theaters. The wealthy elite
and even the stars from those movies fancied being seen and photographed
while playing mini golf.

When the stock market crashed, miniature golf also took a dive. Feeling
financially threatened with the uncertainty, Carter sold all the rights to "Tom
Thumb Golf." The great American miniature golf boom had ended.

Today

On Mackinac Island in Michigan, there is a mini golf course called "The Greens of Mackinac." This is an updated version of Barber's putting course, that now features bent grass putting greens, and a cafe with outdoor seating that overlooks both the greens and Lake Huron.

Yet, with all the upgrades, we will still only need one club, one ball, and sometimes only one shot, to enjoy putting through these gardens.

And as James Barber once told us, this'll do.

JUNIOR GOLF

Have you ever thought to yourself, or have you ever heard someone say, "Boy, I wish I had started to play golf at his age?"

One of the many enjoyable things about learning to play golf at an early age is that you will probably acquire good basic skills that you will be using to play the game for the rest of your life. Golf, when played correctly, is an honorable and self-governing game that should be offered to all children.

OPPORTUNITY AND ENCOURAGEMENT

Opportunity and encouragement are most important in getting juniors interested in the game. Whether they decide to play will be their choice but the initial encouragement is helpful. Unfortunately, some parents push their children so hard that felings of inadequacy cause them to stop playing when they can't perform to the level their parents expect them to.

All children grow and learn at different ages and times. Many juniors will be drawn towards learning the short game, while others will only be interested in hitting the ball far. Allowing them to gravitate towards their preferred interests will expedite their learning to play the game.

POTENTIAL

Recognizing a junior golfer's potential isn't easy, especially if the parents are not golfers. A junior golfer's potential can be viewed in many different ways, and their ability to shoot low scores may not necessarily be that important. Watch how they enjoy playing the game, and their attitude. See how they approach scoring and how they handle their bad shots and bad rounds.

Remember that the only way a junior golfer can fail is to not try, so offer encouragement for every effort regardless of the outcome.

One of the best ways to find the potential of junior's is for them to compete against their peers. Again, they should be given the opportunity to play competitively if that's what they want to do. Many good junior golfers are not immediately interested in competing or playing in tournaments. The stress of competition is not for everyone.

Another question that is often asked is how talented is the junior. Is your golfer just a good player, or does he or she have what it takes to be a great player.

The easiest way to tell if a child is really good will be apparent by their competitive performance.

If a child has the potential to be great, you will not have to ask anyone, because you will be told by everyone.

HOW TO WHIP A GREEN

OLD TOM

Aeration of the soil, especially on putting greens, is an important practice that started in the 1890s. In those days, even with only a few dozen rounds played daily, the St. Andrews Old Course prided itself with maintaining good course conditions. Old Tom Morris, the towns legendary greenskeeper, pioneered the use of sand and top dressing to increase the smoothness and speed of the greens, while continuing to support the natural use of earthworms to aerate the soil; not a popular practice among greenskeepers at the time.

Today, there are more mechanical means of aeration than Old Tom could have ever imagined and with todays demand for perfect putting surfaces, it is no surprise. One popular technique is the use of "tines," or knives, that simply poke holes in the soil. Another modern method used today is to inject ultra high-pressure water through the soil to relieve some compaction. Both of these methods allow the greens to heal quickly, and they are famous for not disrupting play.

CARSON

Carson found the golf course a fascinating place to spend his time. After leaning his bike against the railing on the wooden bridge, he slid down the dirt covered bank, and then giant stepped his way from rock to rock, crossing over and then walking along the bubbling creek that would lead him to the course. His pace quickened when he heard the distant drone of the old work cart's motor getting closer as it bumped and rattled its way across the course. He liked to watch the men when they would cut the greens.

DUDLEY

After parking the cart, the man brought a long, flimsy bamboo pole over to the green. He noticed that little blond haired kid he had seen so many other times standing over by the creek, and today he thought he would reach out to him.

"Want to give it a try?"

Carson grinned, nodded yes, and quickly started walking across the green towards him.

The man reached out his hand saying, "I'm Dudley. What's your name?"

That was the morning Carson learned how to "whip a green."

ARISTOTLE

Dudley showed him how to hold the long tapered pole and how to swish it over the grass so it would slide and not bounce. "The pole knocks the big heavy drops of waters off the tops of the grass, and make them into little drops of water that will seep into the soil," Dudley explained. Then, pointing at the little dirt piles on the green he added, "At the same time, the pole scatters these little mounds of soil the worms make. They're called worm casts."

As he watched Carson sliding the long pole back and forth across the green, Dudley explained that the soil depends on the earthworms and that the tunnels they make in the ground, loosen the soil and allow the water to soak in.

"As they wiggle their way through the dirt they deposit a slime that that acts like vitamins for the soil." Dudley added.

He explained, "The worms eat soil and this other stuff called thatch, grind it up, and then eject it onto the green. The golf courses don't like these castings because they rough up the greens, and that's why we use a bamboo pole to spread out the castings ... there's not much else you can do to get rid of them."

Then he teased Carson saying, "Did you ever hear of a Greek fellow named Aristotle? He nicknamed earthworms the 'intestines of the earth.'" Dudley chuckled when he saw Carson stop whipping, and scrunch up his face making a yucky expression.

Carson stood and watched as Dudley began to mow the green. The self propelled greens mower was more than he could handle right now, but Dudley told him that maybe next year he would show him how to use it.

But for now, Carson would be happy to keep helping Dudley whip the greens . . . and helping those yucky worms too.

Maybe the same way he would have helped Old Tom Morris.

THE CADDIE CUT

It wasn't that long ago that caddies were a big part of the golfing experience. Although a round of golf took only a few hours, the caddies would have to spend a large part of their day waiting around for work. While they waited for the golfers to show up, the caddies would congregate in a small shed-like structure called a caddie shack.

To help pass the time, the caddies would play cards or mumblety-peg, or pitch pennies against the walls of the shack. They would bet on the outcome of these games, with the rule being that all bets would be paid off after caddying.

But a day in the life of a caddie inside a caddie shack isn't just a story about average kids looking for a way to avoid boredom. It is more of a story about young people providing themselves with an opportunity to earn a day's pay while being exposed to a great game that they could learn to play if they had the interest.

Monday was called "caddie's day," and at most golf clubs it was the day caddies were allowed to play on the course. Without having any golf clubs of their own, these caddies would have to borrow clubs from the club's Lost and Found. They would take these borrowed clubs out onto the course and teach themselves how to use them. Through trial and error, they found that they could make up different shots by simply changing the angle of the clubface. They would close the clubface to make the ball run forward, and open the clubface to make the ball land softly and stop quickly.

There is one special golf shot the caddies made up that has been handed down through the years. That shot is called the "caddie cut." It requires that the player take a full swing with a lofted iron and make the ball go higher in the air than it will go forward. The caddie cut is a fun shot when you hit it well, but there is the risk of embarrassment when you miss.

Ideally, the ball must first contact the clubface as it slips underneath it. If you swing the club too low, it will go right under the ball and the ball won't even move. Should your club come in too high, it will catch the ball in the middle and it will fly clear out of sight.

Today, the caddie cut has been renamed and is now called a flop shot.

If you hit a flop shot today, you will be using a lob wedge.

Today, the caddie shack has been renamed and is now called a cart barn.

If you play golf today, you will be using a golf cart.

It wasn't that long ago that caddies were a big part of the golfing experience.

THE PASSING OF HORSHAM VALLEY

"A dying man needs to die, as a sleepy man needs to sleep, and there comes a time when it is wrong, as well as useless, to resist."—Stewart Alsop

We have lost another golf course. Horsham Valley Golf Course in Horsham, Pennsylvania, has been sold and has closed its doors forever. This little course played an important role in our local golf scene by providing a fun and friendly place for all golfers to play.

Golf is not a sport only for the rich, nor is it just for adults. Golf is a game that should welcome anyone's participation, regardless of gender, athletic ability, or physical challenges. Yet kids and first timers have always had trouble finding places to play. This was never the case at Horsham Valley. The mat at the front door said *Welcome*, and the club sincerely meant that. All golfers, including juniors and beginners, were always welcome. The kids were offered golf clinics, golf memberships, golf tournaments, and golf scholarships. They were taught to play the game by the rules and to treat others as they wished to be treated. Learning these life lessons helped many of them on their arduous journey toward becoming mature and successful adults.

The Course

The original course design was created by Scotsman Jock Melville and his son Doug. Then, some thirty years ago, the Melvilles transferred the responsibility of providing "fun golf for all" over to Harry Barbin and Dave Koch. They became the owners and operators of a public golf course, an enviable position for any lover of the game.

Along with the sunshine, though, they had to learn how to handle the droughts and floods. There was the one spring thaw when the winter ice melted away, leaving them with a course covered with rotting turf.

There were so many interesting stories, and so many memorable events. Some of these stories were humorous, and some were unfortunately sad. But still the club seemed blessed with a never-ending cast of characters. These characters not only provided the club with these ongoing and interesting stories, but they usually played the starring role in the stories, too.

The course was often described as "that short, quirky course with all those pine trees," or "it's that course with those small sporty greens." Then someone would try to belittle the course because it was lacking in length, and the regulars would counter with,"If you want it to play long, tee off with your wedge!" The naysayers were always outnumbered, and the little layout was always able to defend itself.

There were frequent charity tournaments, fund raisers, outings, and leagues. There were young moms playing with young kids and old dads playing with old kids. The course was fun to play, and your fun was never compromised. You played Horsham Valley because it was Horsham Valley. If you wanted more, someone would be glad to give you directions to "another type" of course.

Memories

Sadly, there will be houses growing on the land that once grew golfers. It would be calming to think that one day these houses will be leveled, and the land again be made into another golf course. But that won't happen.

And these wonderful things that we now happily remember about Horsham Valley will someday be forgotten.

"And there comes a time when it is wrong, as well as useless, to resist."

But for right now, Horsham Valley, thanks for those memories.

Made in the USA
Charleston, SC
17 December 2013